MAJ SJÖWALL (1935–) and PER WAHLÖÖ (1926–1975) were
husband and wife. They were both committed Marxists and,
between 1965 and 1975, they collaborated on ten mysteries
featuring Martin Beck, including *The Terrorists, The Fire
Engine That Disappeared* and *The Locked Room*. Four of the
books have been made into films, most famously *The
Laughing Policeman*, which starred Walter Matthau.

From the reviews of the *Martin Beck* series:

'First class' — *Daily Telegraph*

'One of the most authentic, gripping and profound
collections of police procedural ever accomplished'

MICHAEL CONNELLY

'Hauntingly effective storytelling' *New York Times*

'There's just no question about it: the reigning King and
Queen of mystery fiction are Maj Sjöwall and her husband
Per Wahlöö' *The National Observer*

'Sjöwall/Wahlöö are the best writers of police procedural in
the world' *Birmingham Post*

Also by Maj Sjöwall and Per Wahlöö

MAJ SJÖWALL
AND PER WAHLÖÖ

The Man on the Balcony

Translated from the Swedish by Alan Blair

HARPER PERENNIAL
London, New York, Toronto and Sydney

Harper Perennial
An imprint of HarperCollins*Publishers*
77–85 Fulham Palace Road
Hammersmith
London W6 8JB

www.harperperennial.co.uk

This edition published by Harper Perennial 2007

1

This translation first published by Random House Inc, New York, in 1968
Originally published in Sweden by P. A. Norstedt & Sönders Förlag

A catalogue record for this book is available from the British Library

This novel is entirely a work of fiction. The names, characters and
incidents portrayed in it are the work of the author's imagination.
Any resemblance to actual persons, living or dead, events or
localities is entirely coincidental.

ISBN 978-0-00-794455-2

Set in Minion by Palimpsest Book Production Limited,
Grangemouth, Stirlingshire

Printed and bound in Great Britain by Clays Ltd, St Ives plc

This is for Barbara and Newton

INTRODUCTION

A man sits on a balcony and watches. A woman watches the man through a pair of binoculars and phones the police.

That is how the novel starts. I first read *The Man on the Balcony* nearly forty years ago. I stumbled across the earlier titles in the Martin Beck series of Maj Sjöwall and Per Wahlöö in my public library. The library was housed in a converted wartime Nissen hut in a small grey town surrounded by a flat, windswept landscape composed largely of black mud and sugar beet. The air inside the hut was a chilly fug smelling of wet raincoats and decaying paper. The librarian was a mournful tweed-covered teddy bear with a matching moustache. Several ladies, grey, plumply corseted and uniformly stern, served as the Gestapo of the establishment, and probably bullied their titular superior as much as they did the borrowers.

As a young teenager, I browsed indiscriminately and greedily. I was often drawn to the yellow jackets of the Gollancz crime list, which was how I found Sjöwall and Wahlöö. Their names were alien and unpronounceable but my elder sister said they were good, so I gave the books a try. A detective story, I thought, must be always a detective story, wherever it came from.

How wrong I was. I soon realized that the novels of Sjöwall and Wahlöö were a world away from the Anglo-American competition, most of which was set either in the sedate precincts of Mayhem Parva, where the blood always washed out of the Vicarage carpet, or in the almost equally cosy environs of a large American city, where law and order was in the hands of a heroic private investigator with a penchant for wisecracking and an unlimited capacity for whiskey.

There was nothing heroic about these books from Sweden. They revealed a strange and uncomfortable place where it was no longer possible to pretend that crime was cosy. They weren't really detective stories, either, or not in the sense I was used to. These were novels about crimes and criminals, detectives and ordinary people. Indeed, they were about crimes whose existence, in some cases, I had not even suspected.

Surely the tweedy teddy bear and the Gestapo ladies could not have been aware of the dangerous contents of these books? This was only a few years after the Lady Chatterley trial. I had already managed to read enough of *Lady Chatterley's Lover* to realize that the fictional universe of Sjöwall and Wahlöö was far more subversive than that of D. H. Lawrence.

Sjöwall and Wahlöö introduced me at an impressionable age to paedophiles, psychopaths, prostitutes, alcoholics, drug addicts, muggers and burglars – here, it seemed, was the sad detritus of humanity. Here too were the police, fallible both as human beings and investigators. As detectives, they groped towards the truth through a fog of ignorance; when they were successful, it was due to hard work and luck rather than forensic brilliance or heroic feats. Above all there was a sense that crime, investigation and punishment were in some fundamental but incomprehensible way linked to the society in which they occurred. Sjöwall and Wahlöö were describing what I should eventually discover was the real world.

Frankly I didn't like it. It was too real for me, too much like the Nissen hut and the smell of wet raincoats and the officious library assistants. At the time, I much preferred Mayhem Parva.

* * *

But time moved on, and so did I. Nearly twenty years later I was making my living by writing my own crime novels, plugging the financial cracks with occasional freelance work for publishers. One of the latter assignments was to advise a crime editor who was considering reissuing selected titles from the Gollancz backlist that extended backwards for half a century. I read – or re-read – with a cynical and essentially professional eye. It was an interesting process, not least because it revealed so much about the changes in crime writing over the years. The puzzle mystery, for example, once the mainstay of the genre, had not worn well, and amateur detectives with amusing personal habits and substantial private incomes were now an endangered species. Most of the books I read could be rejected with a clear conscience.

Then I came to the novels of Sjöwall and Wahlöö. I was struck at once by their enduring quality, and in particular by the combination of relevance and timelessness that is the mark of good fiction. I realized at once that these were more than crime novels: their authors were, quite consciously, using the police procedural to describe and analyse what was, for them, contemporary society; furthermore, their conclusions could be applied to other cities, and other times.

I still have copies of the enthusiastic reports I wrote. Here was part of my assessment of *The Man on the Balcony*: 'The sheer nastiness of it all – of police work in particular and city life in general – comes over very clearly. The themes are obvious, though never overstated: that we are all responsible for crime, since it is a product of the society we have created; and that the police have an ambivalent attitude towards the society they exist to protect.'

Elsewhere I wrote: 'On the surface the book is a sort of minimalist police procedural . . . it is also an excellent novel. The characters are wholly credible, both personally and professionally. The drab Swedish setting is unobtrusively vivid (if that isn't a contradiction in terms). The authors slyly upset our preconceptions about police, crime and criminals – and, by extension, about the nature of the society that engenders them.'

Nowadays we take for granted the availability in English translation of so much excellent Scandinavian crime fiction, from Henning Mankell to Arnaldur Indridason to Gunnar Staalesen. Modern readers have come to relish the sociological perspectives it offers. But even the best examples of it make Sjöwall and Wahlöö's achievement seem still more impressive.

When I first read *The Man on the Balcony*, I had no idea that the series had been planned as a whole, or that the authors had chosen to use the crime novel because, as a literary form, it offered them a unique mechanism for exploring the relationship between the individual and society. By definition, crime novels deal with law-breaking. Laws are the products of their political, economic and cultural contexts; and those who break laws – and uphold them – are constantly both investigating their nature and testing their validity. Sjöwall and Wahlöö, who worked together on the books and wrote alternate chapters, were Communists, and clearly their critique of Swedish society is from a Marxist viewpoint. Fortunately for us, they were also gifted writers, and their novels transcend narrow political philosophy. Taken as a whole, the series is notable for its variety of tone, plot and motivation; it also has moments of surreal comedy.

In terms of fictional chronology, *The Man on the Balcony* is the third title in the series. As a police procedural, its debt to Ed McBain's 87th Precinct novels is obvious. The book's narrative is filtered almost entirely through the team of investigating officers. Martin Beck, now a superintendent, is in operational charge of the case. There are many familiar faces – Inspector Gunvald Larsson, a man whose hearty conviction of his own worth constantly grates on his colleagues; the pipe-smoking Menander with his photographic memory and his need to spend time in the lavatory; Kollberg, the portly former paratrooper who hates violence and refuses to carry a gun, and who in this novel is on the verge of becoming a father for the first time; the delicate Einar Ronn, who's nursing a cold; and Kristiansson and Kvant, the bone-headed patrolmen who pop in and out of the series with the grisly inevitability of a pair of Shakespearean grave-diggers. These are flawed and inconsistent human beings, and much of the authority of both this book and of the series as a whole derives from the fact that the recurring characters are so entirely credible.

It is June 1967 – Sjöwall and Wahlöö are always precise about time and place, true to their journalistic training, just as they are about police procedure. It's shaping up to be a quiet summer in Stockholm, apart from a mugger who, with insolent efficiency, is robbing defenceless citizens in the city's parks and defying police attempts to catch him. Then Martin Beck's tranquillity is ruined when a couple of drunks stumble on the corpse of a nine-year-old girl in one of the parks; she has been sexually assaulted and strangled. Two days later the killer strikes again with the same 'somnambulist certainty'. The only people who might be witnesses are the mugger, whom no one can catch, and a three-year-old boy whom no one can understand. The teeming anonymity of the city hampers the investigation at every turn. The detectives make forays into a grim and degraded underworld of criminals and losers, a place where in a sense everyone is a victim.

The police have ambivalent feelings towards the citizens they are paid to protect. Sometimes, one senses, they prefer uncompli-cated criminals to so-called law-abiding citizens. Respectable 'family men', for example, form a vigilante group to hunt for the killer. Two of them attack Kollberg in a park, and are outraged when he arrests them.

Martin Beck overhears a man holding forth in a tobacconist's: '. . . do you know what they ought to do when they catch this bastard? They ought to execute him in public, they should show it on TV, and they shouldn't do it all at once. No, bit by bit, for several days.' When the man has left, Beck asks who he is. 'His name's Skog,' the tobacconist replies. 'He has the radio workshop next door. Decent chap.'

Decent chaps and family men get their information from the media, which supply their readers and viewers with 'juicy descriptions' of the murders in a socially sanctioned pornography of violence. Brutality is omnipresent and casual. It is hardly worthy of note when, in the course of a police raid, 'a fourteen-year-old schoolgirl was found naked in an attic. She had taken fifty preludin pills and been raped at least twenty times.'

The murderer is eventually caught through a series of trivial events. A police officer remembers a scribble on a telephone directory. A second wants to buy cakes to go with his coffee. A third has a pressing need to urinate before he goes off shift.

It is curious how little the series has dated. *The Man on the Balcony* could almost have been written yesterday. The reader hardly notices that computers are in their infancy, there are no mobile phones, and genetic fingerprinting hasn't yet been invented. (Only the smoking sticks out. Everyone seems to do a great deal of it, including Beck himself; and his wife thinks he's smoking too much on the grounds of cost as much as health.)

There are two reasons for this oddly contemporary quality. One is that the setting is instantly familiar in its essentials: Western cities and the crimes they spawn have changed in forty years, but only in degree, not in kind.

The second reason is that the characters think, speak and act in a way that is instantly and sometimes painfully recognizable. Kollberg loves his heavily pregnant wife but is attracted to a sexually liberated student – until he realizes that the woman reminds him of a corpse he once fancied. Ronn, not the brightest of policemen, simply forgets to mention a vital alibi for a suspect. Larsson – in one of the many moments of unexpected comedy – interrogates a teenage girl about her underwear in the hearing of her middle-class father. A woman watches a man on a balcony because she is in pain and has nothing better to do.

And the man on the balcony watches a nine-year-old girl in a short blue skirt.

Andrew Taylor

1

At a quarter to three the sun rose.

An hour and a half earlier the traffic had thinned out and died away, together with the noise of the last night revellers on their way home. The street-sweeping machines had passed, leaving dark wet strips here and there on the asphalt. An ambulance had wailed down the long, straight street. A black car with white mudguards, radio antenna on the roof and the word POLICE in white block letters on the sides had glided past, silently and slowly. Five minutes later the tinkle of broken glass had been heard as someone drove a gloved hand through a shop window; then came the sound of running footsteps and a car tearing off down a sidestreet.

The man on the balcony had observed all this. The balcony was the ordinary kind with tubular iron rail and sides of corrugated metal. He had stood leaning on the rail, and the glow of his cigarette had been a tiny dark-red spot in the dark. At regular intervals he had stubbed out a cigarette, carefully picked the butt – barely a third of an inch long – out of the wooden holder and placed it beside the others. Ten of these butts were already neatly lined up along the edge of the saucer on the little garden table.

It was quiet now, as quiet as it could be on a mild early summer's night in a big city. A couple of hours still remained before the women who delivered the newspapers appeared, pushing their converted prams, and before the first office cleaner went to work.

The bleak half-light of dawn was dispersed slowly; the first hesitant sunbeams groped over the five-storeyed and six-storeyed blocks of flats and were reflected in the television aerials and the round chimney pots above the roofs on the other side of the street. Then the light fell on the metal roofs themselves, slid quickly down and crept over the eaves along plastered brick walls with rows of unseeing windows, most of which were screened by drawn curtains or lowered Venetian blinds.

The man on the balcony leaned over and looked down the street. It ran from north to south and was long and straight; he could survey a stretch of more than two thousand yards. Once it had been an avenue, a showplace and the pride of the city, but forty years had passed since it was built. The street was almost exactly the same age as the man on the balcony.

When he strained his eyes he could make out a lone figure in the far distance. Perhaps a policeman. For the first time in several hours he went into the flat; he passed through the living room and out into the kitchen. It was broad daylight now and he had no need to switch on the electric light; in fact he used it very sparingly even in the winter. Opening a cupboard, he took out an enamel coffeepot, then measured one and a half cups of water and two spoonfuls of coarse-ground coffee. He put the pot on the stove, struck a match and lit the gas. Felt the match with his fingertips to make sure it had gone out, then opened the door of the cupboard under the sink and threw the dead match into the bin liner. He stood at the stove until the coffee had boiled up, then turned the gas off and went out to the bathroom and urinated while waiting for the grounds to sink. He avoided flushing the toilet so as not to disturb the neighbours. Went back to the kitchen, poured the coffee carefully into the cup, took a lump of sugar from the half-empty packet on the sink and a spoon out of the drawer. Then he carried the cup to the balcony, put it on the varnished wooden table and sat down on the folding chair. The sun had already climbed fairly high and lit up the front of the buildings on the other side of the street down as far as the two lowest flats. Taking a nickel-plated snuffbox from his trouser pocket, he crumbled the cigarette butts one by one, letting the tobacco flakes run through his fingers down into the round metal box and crumpling the bits of paper into pea-sized balls which he placed on the chipped saucer. He stirred the coffee and drank it very slowly. The sirens sounded again, far away. He stood up and watched the ambulance as the howl grew louder and louder and then subsided. A minute later the ambulance was nothing but a small white rectangle which turned left at the north end of the street and vanished from sight. Sitting down again on the folding chair he abstractedly stirred the coffee, which was now cold. He sat quite still, listening to the city wake up around him, at first reluctantly and undecidedly.

The man on the balcony was of average height and normal build. His face was nondescript and he was dressed in a white shirt with no tie, unpressed brown gabardine trousers, grey socks and black shoes. His hair was thin and brushed straight back, he had a big nose and grey-blue eyes.

The time was half past six on the morning of 2 June 1967. The city was Stockholm.

The man on the balcony had no feeling of being observed. He had no particular feeling of anything. He thought he would make some oatmeal a little later.

The street was coming alive. The stream of vehicles was denser and every time the traffic lights at the intersection changed to red the line of waiting cars grew longer. A baker's van tooted angrily at a cyclist who swung out heedlessly into the road. Two cars behind braked with a screech.

The man got up, leaned his arms on the balcony rail and looked down into the street. The cyclist wobbled anxiously in towards the kerb, pretending not to hear the abuse slung at him by the delivery man.

On the pavements a few pedestrians hurried along. Two women in light summer dresses stood talking by the petrol station below the balcony, and farther away a man was exercising his dog. He jerked impatiently at the lead while the dachshund unconcernedly sniffed around the trunk of a tree.

The man on the balcony straightened up, smoothed his thinning hair and put his hands in his pockets. The time now was twenty to eight and the sun was high. He looked up at the sky where a jet plane was drawing a trail of white wool in the blue. Then he lowered his eyes once more to the street and watched an elderly white-haired woman in a pale-blue coat who was standing outside the baker's in the building opposite. She fumbled for a long time in her handbag before getting out a key and unlocking the door. He saw her take out the key, put it in the lock on the inside and then shut the door after her. Drawn down behind the pane of the door was a white blind with the word CLOSED.

At the same moment the door to the flats above the baker's opened and a little girl came out into the sunshine. The man on the balcony moved back a step, took his hands out of his pockets and stood quite still. His eyes were glued to the girl down in the street.

She looked about eight or nine and was carrying a red-checked satchel. She was wearing a short blue skirt, a striped T-shirt and a red jacket with sleeves that were too short. On her feet she had black wooden-soled sandals that made her long thin legs seem even longer and thinner. She turned to the left outside the door and started walking slowly along the street with lowered head.

The man on the balcony followed her with his eyes. When she had gone about twenty yards she stopped, raised her hand to her breast and stood like that for a moment. Then she opened the satchel and rummaged in it while she turned and began to walk

4

back. Then she broke into a run and rushed back inside without closing the satchel.

The man on the balcony stood quite still and watched the entrance door close behind her. Some minutes passed before it opened again and the girl came out. She had closed the satchel now and walked more quickly. Her fair hair was tied in a pony tail and swung against her back. When she got to the end of the block she turned the corner and disappeared.

The time was three minutes to eight. The man turned around, went inside and into the kitchen. There he drank a glass of water, rinsed the glass, put it on the rack and went out again on to the balcony.

He sat down on the folding chair and laid his left arm on the rail. He lit a cigarette and looked down into the street while he smoked.

2

The time by the electric wall-clock was five minutes to eleven and the date, according to the calendar on Gunvald Larsson's desk, was Friday, 2 June 1967.

Martin Beck was only in the room by chance. He had just come in and put down his case on the floor inside the door. He had said hello, laid his hat beside the carafe on the filing cabinet, taken a glass from the tray and filled it with water, leaned against the cabinet and was about to drink. The man behind the desk looked at him ill-humouredly and said:

'Have they sent you here too? What have we done wrong now?'

Martin Beck took a sip of water.

'Nothing, as far as I know. And don't worry. I only came up to see Melander. I asked him to do something for me. Where is he?'

'In the lavatory as usual.'

Melander's curious capacity for always being in the lavatory was a hackneyed joke, and although there was a grain of truth in it Martin Beck for some reason felt irritated.

Mostly, however, he kept his irritation to himself. He gave the man at the desk a calm, searching look and said:

'What's bothering you?'

6

'What do you think? The muggings of course. There was one in Vanadis Park last night again.'

'So I heard.'

'A pensioner who was out with his dog. Struck on the head from behind. A hundred and forty kronor in his wallet. Concussion. Still in hospital. Heard nothing. Saw nothing.'

Martin Beck was silent.

'This was the eighth time in two weeks. That guy will end by killing someone.'

Martin Beck drained the glass and put it down.

'If someone doesn't grab him soon,' Gunvald Larsson said.

'Who do you mean by someone?'

'The police, for Christ's sake. Us. Anybody. A civil patrol from the protection squad in ninth district was there ten minutes before it happened.'

'And when it happened? Where were they then?'

'Sitting over coffee at the station. It's the same all the time. If there's a policeman hiding in every bush in Vanadis Park, then it happens in Vasa Park, and if there's a policeman hiding in every bush in both Vanadis Park and Vasa Park, then he pops up in Lill-Jans Wood.'

'And if there's a policeman in every bush there too?'

'Then the demonstrators break up the US Trade Centre and set fire to the American embassy. This is no joking matter,' Gunvald Larsson added stiffly.

Keeping his eyes fixed on him, Martin Beck said:

'I'm not joking. I just wondered.'

'This man knows his business. It's almost as if he had radar. There's never a policeman in sight when he attacks.'

Martin Beck rubbed the bridge of his nose between thumb and forefinger.

'Send out . . .'

Larsson broke in at once.

'Send out? Whom? What? The dog van? And let those damn

dogs tear the civil patrol to pieces? Yesterday's victim had a dog, come to that. What good was it to him?'

'What kind of dog?'

'How the hell do I know? Shall I interrogate the dog perhaps? Shall I get the dog here and send it out to the lavatory so that Melander can interrogate it?'

Gunvald Larsson said this with great gravity. He pounded the desk with his fist and went on:

'A lunatic prowls about the parks bashing people on the head and you come here and start talking about dogs!'

'Actually it wasn't I who . . .'

Again Gunvald Larsson interrupted him.

'Anyway, I told you, this man knows his business. He only goes for defenceless old men and women. And always from behind. What was it someone said last week? Oh yes, "he leaped out of the bushes like a panther."'

'There's only one way,' Martin Beck said in a honeyed voice.

'What's that?'

'You'd better go out yourself. Disguised as a defenceless old man.'

The man at the desk turned his head and glared at him.

Gunvald Larsson was six foot three and weighed fifteen and a half stone. He had shoulders like a heavyweight boxer and huge hands covered with shaggy blond hair. He had fair hair, brushed straight back, and discontented, clear blue eyes. Kollberg usually completed the description by saying that the expression on his face was that of a motorcyclist.

Just now the blue eyes were looking at Martin Beck with more than the usual disapproval.

Martin Beck shrugged and said:

'Joking apart . . .'

And Gunvald Larsson interrupted him at once.

'Joking apart I can't see anything funny in this. Here am I up to my neck in one of the worst cases of robbery I've ever known, and along you come drivelling about dogs and God knows what.'

Martin Beck realized that the other man, no doubt unintentionally, was about to do something that only few succeeded in: to annoy him to the point of making him lose his temper. And although he was quite well aware of this, he could not help raising his arm from the cabinet and saying:

'That's enough!'

At that moment, fortunately, Melander came in from the room next door. He was in his shirtsleeves, and had a pipe in his mouth and an open telephone directory in his hands.

'Hello,' he said.

'Hello,' said Martin Beck.

'I thought of the name the second you hung up,' Melander said. 'Arvid Larsson. Found him in the telephone directory too. But it's no good calling him. He died in April. Stroke. But he was in the same line of business up to the last. Had a rag-and-bone shop on the south side. It's shut now.'

Martin Beck took the directory, looked at it and nodded. Melander dug a matchbox out of his trouser pocket and began elaborately lighting his pipe. Martin Beck took two steps into the room and put the directory down on the table. Then he went back to the filing cabinet.

'What are you busy on, you two?' Gunvald Larsson asked suspiciously.

'Nothing much,' Melander said. 'Martin had forgotten the name of a fence we tried to nab twelve years ago.'

'And did you?'

'No,' said Melander.

'But you remembered it?'

'Yes.'

Gunvald Larsson pulled the directory towards him, riffled through it and said:

'How the devil can you remember the name of a man called Larsson for twelve years?'

9

'It's quite easy,' Melander said gravely.

The telephone rang.

'First division, duty officer.

'Sorry, madam, what did you say?

'What?

'Am I a detective? This is the duty officer of the first division, Detective Inspector Larsson.

'And your name is . . . ?'

Gunvald Larsson took a ball-point pen from his breast pocket and scribbled a word. Then sat with the pen in mid-air.

'And what can I do for you?

'Sorry, I didn't get that.

'Eh? A what?

'A cat?

'A cat on the balcony?

'Oh, a man.

'Is there a man standing on your balcony?'

Gunvald Larsson pushed the telephone directory aside and drew a memo pad towards him. Put pen to paper. Wrote a few words.

'Yes, I see. What does he look like, did you say?

'Yes, I'm listening. Thin hair brushed straight back. Big nose. Aha. White shirt. Average height. Hm. Brown trousers. Unbuttoned. What? Oh, the shirt. Blue-grey eyes.

'One moment, madam. Let's get this straight. You mean he's standing on his own balcony?'

Gunvald Larsson looked from Melander to Martin Beck and shrugged. He went on listening and poked his ear with the pen.

'Sorry, madam. You say this man is standing on his own balcony? Has he molested you?

'Oh, he hasn't. What? On the other side of the street? On his own balcony?

'Then how can you see that he has blue-grey eyes? It must be a very narrow street.

'What? You're doing what?

'Now wait a minute, madam. All this man has done is to stand on his own balcony. What else is he doing?

'Looking down into the street? What's happening in the street?

'Nothing? What did you say? Cars? Children playing?

'At night too? Do the children play at night too?

'Oh, they don't. But he stands there at night? What do you want us to do? Send the dog van?

'As a matter of fact there's no law forbidding people to stand on their balconies, madam.

'Report an observation, you say? Heavens above, madam, if everyone reported their observations we'd need three policemen for every inhabitant.

'Grateful? We ought to be grateful?

'Impertinent? I've been impertinent? Now look here, madam . . .'

Gunvald Larsson broke off and sat with the receiver a foot from his ear.

'She hung up,' he said in amazement.

After three seconds he banged down the receiver and said:

'Go to hell, you old bitch.'

He tore off the sheet of paper he had been writing on and carefully wiped the ear wax off the tip of the pen.

'People are crazy,' he said. 'No wonder we get nothing done. Why doesn't the switchboard block calls like that? There ought to be a direct line to the nut house.'

'You'll just have to get used to it,' Melander said, calmly taking his telephone directory, closing it and going into the next room.

Gunvald Larsson, having finished cleaning his pen, crumpled up the paper and tossed it into the wastepaper basket. With a sour look at the suitcase by the door he said:

'Where are you off to?'

'Just going down to Motala for a couple of days,' Martin Beck replied. 'Something there I must look at.'

'Oh.'

11

'Be back inside a week. But Kollberg will be home today. He's on duty here as from tomorrow. So you needn't worry.'

'I'm not worrying.'

'By the way, those robberies . . .'

'Yes?'

'No, it doesn't matter.'

'If he does it twice more we'll get him,' Melander said from the next room.

'Exactly,' said Martin Beck. 'So long.'

'So long,' Gunvald Larsson replied.

3

Martin Beck got to Central Station nineteen minutes before the train was due to leave and thought he would fill in the time by making two telephone calls.

First home.

'Haven't you left yet?' his wife said.

He ignored this rhetorical question and merely said:

'I'll be staying at a hotel called the Palace. Thought you'd better know.'

'How long will you be away?'

'A week.'

'How do you know for certain?'

This was a good question. She wasn't dumb at any rate, Martin Beck thought.

'Love to the children,' he said, adding after a moment, 'take care of yourself.'

'Thanks,' she said coldly.

He hung up and fished another coin out of his trouser pocket. There was a line in front of the telephone boxes and the people standing nearest glared at him as he put the coin in the slot and dialled the number of southern police headquarters. It took about a minute before he got Kollberg on the line.

'Beck here. Just wanted to make sure you were back.'

'Very thoughtful of you,' Kollberg said. 'Are you still here?'

'How's Gun?'

'Fine. Big as a house of course.'

Gun was Kollberg's wife; she was expecting a baby at the end of August.

'I'll be back in a week.'

'So I gather. And by that time I shall no longer be on duty here.' There was a pause, then Kollberg said:

'What takes you to Motala?'

'That fellow . . .'

'Which fellow?'

'That second-hand dealer who was burned to death the night before last. Haven't you . . .'

'I read about it in the papers. So what?'

'I'm going down to have a look.'

'Are they so dumb they can't clear up an ordinary fire on their own?'

'Anyway they've asked . . .'

'Look here,' Kollberg said. 'You might get your wife to swallow that, but you can't kid me. Anyway, I know quite well what they've asked and who has asked it. Who's head of the investigation department at Motala now?'

'Ahlberg, but . . .'

'Exactly. I also know that you've taken five vacation days that were due to you. In other words you're going to Motala in order to sit and tipple at the City Hotel with Ahlberg. Am I right?'

'Well . . .'

'Good luck,' Kollberg said genially. 'Behave yourself.'

'Thanks.'

Martin Beck hung up and the man standing behind him elbowed his way roughly past him. Beck shrugged and went out into the main hall of the station.

Kollberg was right up to a point. This in itself didn't matter in the least, but it was vexing all the same to be seen through so easily. Both he and Kollberg had met Ahlberg in connection with a murder case three summers earlier. The investigation had been long and difficult and in the course of it they had become good friends. Otherwise Ahlberg would hardly have asked the national police board for help and he himself would not have wasted half a day's work on the case.

The station clock showed that the two telephone calls had taken exactly four minutes; there was still a quarter of an hour before the train left. As usual the big hall was swarming with people of all kinds.

Suitcase in hand, he stood there glumly, a man of medium height with a lean face, a broad forehead and a strong jaw. Most of those who saw him probably took him for a bewildered provincial who suddenly found himself in the rush and bustle of the big city.

'Hi, mister,' someone said in a hoarse whisper.

He turned to look at the person who had accosted him. A girl in her early teens was standing beside him; she had lank fair hair and was wearing a short batik dress. She was barefoot and dirty and looked the same age as his own daughter. In her cupped right hand she was holding a strip of four photographs, which she let him catch a glimpse of.

It was very easy to trace these pictures. The girl had gone into one of the automatic photo machines, knelt on the stool, pulled her dress up to her armpits and fed her coins into the slot.

The curtains of these photo cubicles had been shortened to knee height, but it didn't seem to have helped much. He glanced at the pictures; young girls these days developed earlier than they used to, he thought. And the little slobs never thought of wearing anything underneath either. All the same, the photos had not come out very well.

'Twenty-five kronor?' the child said hopefully.

Martin Beck looked around in annoyance and caught sight of

two policemen in uniform on the other side of the hall. He went over to them. One of them recognized him and saluted.

'Can't you keep the kids here in order?' Martin Beck said angrily.

'We do our best, sir.'

The policeman who answered was the same one who had saluted, a young man with blue eyes and a fair, well-trimmed beard.

Martin Beck said nothing but turned and walked towards the glass doors leading out to the platforms. The girl in the batik dress was now standing farther down the hall, looking furtively at the pictures, wondering if there was something wrong with her appearance.

Before long some idiot was sure to buy her photographs.

Then off she would go to Humlegården or Mariatorget and buy purple hearts or marijuana with the money. Or perhaps LSD.

The policeman who recognized him had had a beard. Twenty-four years earlier, when he himself joined the force, policemen had not worn beards.

By the way, why hadn't the other policeman saluted, the one without a beard? Because he hadn't recognized him?

Twenty-four years ago policemen had saluted anyone who came up to them even if he were not a superintendent. Or had they?

In those days girls of fourteen and fifteen had not photographed themselves naked in photo machines and tried to sell the pictures to detective superintendents in order to get money for a fix.

Anyway, he was not a bit pleased with the new title he had got at the beginning of the year. He was not pleased with his new office at southern police headquarters out in the noisy industrial area at Västberga. He was not pleased with his suspicious wife and with the fact that someone like Gunvald Larsson could be made a detective inspector.

Martin Beck sat by the window in his first-class compartment, pondering all this.

The train glided out of the station and past the City Hall. He caught sight of the old white steamer *Mariefred*, that still plied to Gripsholm, and the publishing house of Norstedt, before the train was swallowed up in the tunnel to the south. When it emerged into daylight again he saw the green expanse of Tantolunden – the park that he was soon going to have nightmares about – and heard the wheels echo on the railway bridge.

By the time the train stopped at Södertälje he was in a better mood. He bought a bottle of mineral water and a stale cheese sandwich from the metal handcart that now replaced the restaurant car on most of the express trains.

4

'Well,' Ahlberg said, 'that's how it happened. It was rather chilly that night and he had one of those old-fashioned electric heaters that he stood beside the bed. Then he kicked off the blanket in his sleep and it fell down over the heater and caught fire.'

Martin Beck nodded.

'It seems quite plausible,' Ahlberg said. 'The technical investigation was completed today. I tried to phone you but you had already left.'

They were standing on the site of the fire at Borenshult and between the trees they could glimpse the lake and the flight of locks where they had found a dead woman three years earlier. All that remained of the burned-down house were the foundation and the base of the chimney. The fire brigade had, however, managed to save a small outhouse.

'There were some stolen goods there,' Ahlberg said. 'He was a fence, this fellow Larsson. But he'd been sentenced before, so we weren't surprised. We'll send out a list of the things.'

Martin Beck nodded again, then said:

'I checked up on his brother in Stockholm. He died last spring. Stroke. He was a fence too.'

'Seems to have run in the family,' Ahlberg said.

'The brother never got caught but Melander remembered him.'

'Oh yes, Melander . . . he's like the elephant, he never forgets. You don't work together any more, do you?'

'Only sometimes. He's at headquarters in Kungsholmsgatan. Kollberg too, as from today. It's crazy, the way they keep moving us about.'

They turned their backs on the scene of the fire and went back to the car in silence.

A quarter of an hour later Ahlberg drew up in front of the police station, a low yellow-brick building at the corner of Prästgatan and Kungsgatan, just near the main square and the statue of Baltzar von Platen. Half-turning to Martin Beck he said:

'Now that you're here with nothing to do you might as well stay for a couple of days.'

Martin Beck nodded.

'We can go out with the motorboat,' Ahlberg said.

That evening they dined at the City Hotel on the local speciality from Lake Vättern, a delicious salmon trout. They also had a few drinks.

On Saturday they took the motorboat out on the lake. On Sunday too. On Monday Martin Beck borrowed the motorboat. And again on Tuesday. On Wednesday he went to Vadstena and had a look at the castle.

The hotel he was staying at in Motala was modern and comfortable. He got on well with Ahlberg. He read a novel by Kurt Salomonson called *The Man Outside*. He was enjoying himself.

He deserved it. He had worked very hard during the winter and the spring had been awful. The hope that it would be a quiet summer still remained.

5

The mugger had nothing against the weather.

It had started to rain early in the afternoon. At first heavily, then in a steady drizzle which had stopped about seven o'clock. But the sky was still overcast and oppressive and the rain was obviously going to start again soon. It was now nine o'clock and dusk was spreading under the trees. Half an hour or so still remained before lighting-up time.

The mugger had taken off his thin plastic raincoat and laid it beside him on the park bench. He was wearing tennis shoes, khaki trousers and a neat grey nylon pullover with a monogram on the breast pocket. A large red bandanna handkerchief was tied loosely around his neck. He had been in the park or its immediate vicinity for over two hours, observing people closely and calculatingly. On two occasions he had studied the passers-by with special interest and each time it had been not one person but two. The first couple had been a young man and a girl; both were younger than himself, the girl was dressed in sandals and a short black-and-white summer dress, the boy wore a smart blazer and light-grey trousers. They had made their way to the shady paths in the most secluded corner of the park. There they had stopped and embraced. The girl had stood with her back to a tree and after only a few seconds the boy had thrust his right hand up under her skirt and inside the elastic band of her panties and started digging with his fingers between her legs. 'Someone might come,' she said mechanically, but she had immediately moved her feet apart. The next second she had closed her eyes and started to twist her hips rhythmically, at the same time scratching the back of the boy's well-trimmed neck with the fingers of her left hand. What she had done with her right hand he had not been able to see, although he had been so close to them that he had caught a glimpse of the white lace panties.

He had walked on the grass, following them with silent steps, and stood crouched behind the bushes less than a dozen yards away. He had carefully weighed the pros and cons. An attack appealed to his sense of humour, but on the other hand the girl had no handbag and also he might not be able to stop her from screaming, which in its turn might impede the practice of his profession. Besides, the boy looked stronger and broader across the shoulders than he had first thought, and anyway it wasn't at all certain that he had any money in his wallet. An attack seemed unwise, so he had crept away as silently as he had come. He was no Peeping Tom, he had more important things to do; in any case, he presumed there wasn't much more to see. Before long the young couple had left the park, now suitably far apart. They had crossed the street and entered a block of flats, the outside of which indicated stable middle-class respectability. In the doorway the girl had straightened her panties and bra and drawn a moistened fingertip along her eyebrows. The boy had combed his hair.

At half past eight his attention focused on the next two people. A red Volvo had stopped in front of the ironmongers at the street corner. Two men were in the front seat. One of them got out and went into the park. He was bareheaded and wore a beige-coloured raincoat. A few minutes later the second man had got out and gone into the park another way; he was wearing a cap and tweed jacket but had no overcoat. After about fifteen minutes they had

21

returned to the car, from different directions and at an interval of some minutes. He had stood with his back to them, looking into the window of the ironmongers, and he had overheard clearly what they said.

'Well?'

'Nothing.'

'What do we do now?'

'Lill-Jans Wood?'

'In this weather?'

'Well . . .'

'Okay. But then we have coffee.'

'Okay.'

They had banged the car doors and driven off.

And now it was nearly nine o'clock and he sat on the bench waiting.

He caught sight of her as soon as she entered the park and knew at once which path she would take. A dumpy, middle-aged woman with overcoat, umbrella and large handbag. Looked promising. Maybe she kept a fruit and tobacco kiosk. He got up and put on the plastic raincoat, cut across the lawn and crouched down behind the bushes. She came on along the path, was almost abreast of him now – in five seconds, perhaps ten. With his left hand he drew the bandanna handkerchief up over his nose and thrust the fingers of his right hand into the brass knuckles. She was only a few yards away now. He moved swiftly and his footsteps on the wet grass were almost silent.

But only almost. He was still a yard behind the woman when she turned around, saw him and opened her mouth to scream. Unreflectingly he struck her across the mouth as hard as he could. He heard a crunch. The woman dropped her umbrella and staggered, then fell to her knees, clutching her handbag with both hands as if she had a baby to protect.

He struck her again, and her nose crunched under the brass knuckles. She fell back, her legs doubled under her, and didn't utter a sound. She was streaming with blood and seemed hardly conscious, but all the same he took a handful of sand from the path and strewed it over her eyes. At the same instant that he tore open the handbag her head flopped to one side, her jaw fell open, and she started to vomit.

Handbag, purse, a wrist watch. Not so bad.

The mugger was already on his way out of the park. As if she'd been protecting a baby, he thought. It could have been such a nice neat job. The silly old bitch.

A quarter of an hour later he was home. The time was half past nine on the evening of 9 June 1967, a Friday. Twenty minutes later it started to rain.

6

It rained all night but on Saturday morning the sun was shining again, hidden only now and then by the fluffy white clouds that floated across the clear blue sky. It was 10 June, the summer holidays had begun, and on Friday evening long lines of cars had crawled out of town on their way to country cottages, boat jetties and camping sites. But the city was still full of people who, as the weekend promised to be fine, would have to make do with the makeshift country life offered by parks and open-air swimming pools.

The time was a quarter past nine and a line was already waiting outside the pay window of the Vanadis Baths. Sun-thirsty Stockholmers, craving a swim, streamed up the paths leading from Sveavägen.

Two seedy figures crossed Frejgatan against the red light. One was dressed in jeans and a pullover, the other in black trousers and a brown jacket which bulged suspiciously over the left-hand breast pocket. They walked slowly, peering bleary-eyed against the sun. The man with the bulge in his jacket staggered and nearly bumped into a cyclist, an athletic man of sixty or so in a light-grey summer suit, with a pair of wet swimming trunks on the baggage carrier. The cyclist wobbled and had to put one foot to the ground.

'Clumsy idiots!' he shouted, as he rode pompously away.

'Stupid old fool,' the man with the jacket said. 'Looks like a damned millionaire. Why, he might have knocked me down. I might have fallen and broken the bottle.'

He stopped indignantly on the pavement and the mere thought of how near he had been to disaster made him shudder and raise his hand to the bottle in his jacket.

'And do you think he'd have paid for it? Not likely. Sitting pretty, he is, in a swanky apartment at Norr Mälarstrand with his fridge full of champagne, but the sonofabitch wouldn't think of paying for some poor bloke's bottle of booze that he'd broken. Dirty bastard!'

'But he didn't break it,' his friend objected quietly.

The second man was much younger; he took his irate companion by the arm and piloted him into the park. They climbed the slope, not towards the pool like the others but on past the gates. Then they turned off on to the path leading from Stefan's Church to the top of the hill. It was a steep pull and they were soon out of breath. Halfway up the younger man said:

'Sometimes you can find a few coins in the grass behind the tower. If they've been playing poker there the night before. We might scrape enough together for another half-bottle before the off licence closes . . .'

It was Saturday and the off licences shut at one o'clock.

'Not a hope. It was raining yesterday.'

'So it was,' the younger man said with a sigh.

The path skirted the fence of the bathing enclosure, which was teeming with bathers, some of them tanned so dark that they looked like Negroes, some of them real Negroes, but most of them pale after a long winter without even a week in the Canary Islands.

'Hey, wait a minute,' the younger man said. 'Let's have a look at the girls.'

The older man walked on, saying over his shoulder:

'Hell, no. Come on, I'm as thirsty as a camel.'

They went on up towards the water tower at the top of the park. Having rounded the gloomy building, they saw to their relief that they had the ground behind the tower to themselves. The older man sat down in the grass, took out the bottle and started unscrewing the cap. The younger man had continued to the top of the slope on the other side, where a red-painted wooden fence sagged.

'Jocke!' he shouted. 'Let's sit here instead. In case anyone comes.'

Jocke got up, wheezing, and bottle in hand followed the other man, who had started down the slope.

'Here's a good spot,' the younger man called, 'by these bush . . .'

He stopped dead and bent forward.

'Christ!' he whispered hoarsely. 'Jesus Christ!'

Jocke came up behind him, saw the girl on the ground, turned aside and vomited.

She was lying with the top part of her body half hidden under a bush. Her legs, wide apart, were stretched out on the damp sand. The face, turned to one side, was bluish and the mouth was open. Her right arm was bent over her head and her left hand lay against her hip, palm upwards.

The fair, longish hair had fallen across her cheek. She was barefoot and dressed in a skirt and a striped cotton T-shirt that had slipped up, leaving her waist bare.

She had been about nine years old.

There was no doubt that she was dead.

The time was five minutes to ten when Jocke and his mate appeared at the ninth district police station in Surbrunnsgatan. They gave a rambling and nervous account of what they had seen in Vanadis Park to a police inspector called Granlund, who was duty officer. Ten minutes later Granlund and four policemen were on the spot.

Only twelve hours had passed since two of the four policemen

26

had been called to an adjacent part of the park, where yet another brutal robbery had taken place. As nearly an hour had passed between the assault and the time it was reported, everyone had taken it for granted that the assailant had made himself scarce. They had therefore not examined the area closely and couldn't say whether the girl's body had been there at that time or not.

The five policemen established the fact that the girl was dead and that as far as they could tell she had been strangled. That was about all they could do for the moment.

While waiting for the detectives and the men from the technical department their main duty was to see that no busybodies came prying about.

Granlund, casting his eye over the scene of the crime, saw that the men from headquarters were not going to have an easy job. It had obviously rained heavily for some time after the body had been put there. On the other hand he thought he knew who the girl was, and the knowledge didn't make him too happy.

At eleven o'clock the previous evening an anxious mother had come to the police station and begged them to search for her daughter. The girl was eight and a half years old. She had gone out to play at about seven, and had not been heard of since. The ninth district had alerted headquarters and all men on patrol had been given the girl's description. The accident wards of all hospitals had been checked.

The description, unfortunately, seemed to fit.

As far as Granlund knew, the missing girl had not been found. Also, she lived in Sveavägen near Vanadis Park. There seemed no room for doubt.

He thought of the girl's parents waiting at home in suspense, and inwardly he prayed that he would not have to be the one who told them the truth.

When the detectives at last arrived Granlund felt as if he had

27

been standing an eternity in the sunshine near the child's little body.

As soon as the experts began their work he left them to it and walked back to the police station, the image of the dead girl branded on his retina.

7

When Kollberg and Rönn reached the scene of the crime in Vanadis Park the area behind the water tower was properly roped off. The photographer had finished his work and the doctor was busy with his first routine examination of the body.

The ground was still damp and the only footprints near the body were fresh and had almost certainly been made by the men who had found the body. The girl's sandals were lying farther down the slope near the red fence.

When the doctor had finished Kollberg went up to him and said, 'Well?'

'Strangled,' the doctor said. 'Rape of some sort. Maybe.'

He shrugged.

'When?'

'Last evening some time. Find out when she last ate and what . . .'

'I know. Do you think it happened here?'

'I see no signs that it didn't.'

'No,' Kollberg said. 'Why the hell did it have to rain like that.'

'Huh,' the doctor said, walking off towards his car.

Kollberg stayed for another half hour, then took a car from the ninth district to the station at Surbrunnsgatan.

The superintendent was at his desk reading a report when Kollberg entered. He greeted him and put the report aside. Pointed to a chair. Kollberg sat down and said:

'Nasty business.'

'Yes,' the superintendent said. 'Have you found anything?'

'Not as far as I know. I think the rain has ruined everything.'

'When do you think it happened? We had an assault case up there last evening. I was just looking at the report.'

'I don't know,' Kollberg said. 'We'll see when we can move her.'

'Do you think it can be the same guy? That she saw him do it, or something?'

'If she has been raped it's hardly the same one. A mugger who is also a sex murderer . . . it's a bit much,' Kollberg said vaguely.

'Raped? Did the doctor say so?'

'He thought it possible.'

Kollberg sighed and rubbed his chin.

'The boys who drove me here said you know who she is.'

'Yes,' the superintendent said. 'It seems like it. Granlund was in just now and identified her from a photo her mother brought in here last night.'

The superintendent opened a file, took out a snapshot and gave it to Kollberg. The girl who now lay dead in Vanadis Park was leaning against a tree and laughing up at the sun. Kollberg nodded and handed the photo back.

'Do the parents know that . . .'

'No,' the superintendent said.

He tore a sheet off the note pad in front of him and gave it to Kollberg.

'Mrs Karin Carlsson, Sveavägen 83,' Kollberg read aloud.

'The girl's name was Eva,' the superintendent said. 'Someone had better . . . you had better go there. Now. Before she finds out in a more unpleasant way.'

'It's quite unpleasant enough as it is,' Kollberg sighed.

The superintendent regarded him gravely but said nothing.

'Anyway, I thought this was your district,' Kollberg said. But he stood up and continued:

'Okay, okay, I'll go. Someone has to do it.'

In the doorway he turned and said:

'No wonder we're short of men in the force. You have to be crazy to become a cop.'

As he had left his car by Stefan's Church he decided to walk to Sveavägen. Besides, he wanted to take his time before meeting the girl's parents.

The sun was shining and all traces of the night's rain had already dried up. Kollberg felt slightly sick at the thought of the task ahead of him. It was disagreeable, to say the least. He had been forced into similar tasks before, but now, in the case of a child, the ordeal was worse than ever. If only Martin had been here, he thought; he's much better at this sort of thing than I am. Then he remembered how depressed Martin Beck had always seemed in situations like this, and followed up the train of thought: hah, it's just as hard for everyone, whoever has to do it.

The block of flats where the dead girl had lived was obliquely opposite Vanadis Park, between Surbrunnsgatan and Frejgatan. The lift was out of order and he had to walk up the five flights. He stood still for a moment and got his breath before ringing the doorbell.

The woman opened the door almost at once. She was dressed in a brown cotton housecoat and sandals. Her fair hair was tousled, as if she had been pushing her fingers through it over and over again. When she saw Kollberg her face fell with disappointment, then her expression hovered between hope and fear.

Kollberg showed his identity card and she gave him a desperate, inquiring look.

'May I come in?'

The woman opened the door wide and stepped back.

'Haven't you found her?' she said.

Kollberg walked in without answering. The flat seemed to

consist of two rooms. The outer one contained a bed, bookshelves, desk, TV set, chest of drawers and two armchairs, one on each side of a low teak table. The bed was made, presumably no one had slept in it that night. On the blue bedspread was a suitcase, open, and beside it lay piles of neatly folded clothes. A couple of newly ironed cotton dresses hung over the lid of the suitcase. The door of the inner room was open; Kollberg caught sight of a blue-painted bookshelf with books and toys. On top sat a white teddy bear.

'Do you mind if we sit down?' Kollberg asked, and sat in one of the armchairs.

The woman remained standing and said:

'What has happened? Have you found her?'

Kollberg saw the dread and the panic in her eyes and tried to keep quite calm.

'Yes,' he said. 'Please sit down, Mrs Carlsson. Where is your husband?'

She sat in the armchair opposite Kollberg.

'I have no husband. We're divorced. Where's Eva? What has happened?'

'Mrs Carlsson, I'm terribly sorry to tell you this. Your daughter is dead.'

The woman stared at him.

'No,' she said. 'No.'

Kollberg got up and went over to her.

'Have you no one who can be with you? Your parents?'

The woman shook her head.

'It's not true,' she said.

Kollberg put his hand on her shoulder.

'I'm terribly sorry, Mrs Carlsson,' he said lamely.

'But how? We were going to the country ...'

'We're not sure yet,' Kollberg replied. 'We think that she ... that she's been the victim of ...'

'Killed? Murdered?'

32

Kollberg nodded.

The woman shut her eyes and sat stiff and still. Then she opened her eyes and shook her head.

'Not Eva,' she said. 'It's not Eva. You haven't . . . you've made a mistake.'

'No,' Kollberg said. 'I can't tell you how sorry I am, Mrs Carlsson. Isn't there anyone I can call? Someone I can ask to come here? Your parents or someone?'

'No, no, not them. I don't want anyone here.'

'Your ex-husband?'

'He's living in Malmö, I think.'

Her face was ashen and her eyes were hollow. Kollberg saw that she had not yet grasped what had happened, that she had put up a mental barrier which would not allow the truth past it. He had seen the same reaction before and knew that when she could no longer resist, she would collapse.

'Who is your doctor, Mrs Carlsson?' Kollberg asked.

'Doctor Ström. We were there on Wednesday. Eva had had a tummy ache for several days and as we were going to the country I thought I'd better . . .'

She broke off and looked at the doorway into the other room.

'Eva's never sick as a rule. And she soon got over this tummy ache. The doctor thought it was a touch of gastric flu.'

She sat silent for a moment. Then she said, so softly that Kollberg could hardly catch the words:

'She's all right again now.'

Kollberg looked at her, feeling desperate and idiotic. He did not know what to say or do. She was still sitting with her face turned towards the open door into her daughter's room. He was trying frantically to think of something to say when she suddenly got up and called her daughter's name in a loud, shrill voice. Then she ran into the other room. Kollberg followed her.

The room was bright and nicely furnished. In one corner stood a red-painted box full of toys and at the foot of the narrow bed was an old-fashioned doll's house. A pile of schoolbooks lay on the desk.

The woman was sitting on the edge of the bed, her elbows propped on her knees and face buried in her hands. She rocked to and fro and Kollberg could not hear whether she was crying or not.

He looked at her for a moment, then went out into the hall where he had seen the telephone. An address book lay beside it and in it, sure enough, he found Doctor Ström's number.

The doctor listened while Kollberg explained the situation and promised to come within five minutes.

Kollberg went back to the woman, who was sitting as he had left her. She was making no sound. He sat down beside her and waited. At first he wondered whether he dared touch her, but after a while he put his arm cautiously around her shoulders. She seemed unaware of his presence.

They sat like this until the silence was broken by the doctor's ring at the door.

8

Kollberg was sweating as he walked back through Vanadis Park. The cause was neither the steep incline, the humid heat after the rain, nor his tendency to corpulence. At any rate not entirely.

Like most of those who were to deal with this case, he was jaded before the investigation started. He thought of the repulsiveness of the crime itself and he thought of the people who had been so hard hit by its blind meaninglessness. He had been through all this before, how many times he couldn't even say offhand, and he knew exactly how horrible it could turn out to be. And how difficult.

He thought too of the swift gangsterization of this society, which in the last resort must be a product of himself and of the other people who lived in it and had a share in its creation. He thought of the rapid technical expansion that the police force had undergone merely during the last year; despite this, crime always seemed to be one step ahead. He thought of the new investigation methods and the computers, which could mean that this particular criminal might be caught within a few hours, and also what little consolation these excellent technical inventions had to offer the woman he had just left, for example. Or himself. Or the set-faced men who had now gathered around the little body in the bushes between the rocks and the red fence.

He had only seen the body for a few moments, and at a distance, and he didn't want to see it again if he could help it. This he knew to be an impossibility. The mental image of the child in the blue skirt and striped T-shirt was etched into his mind and would always remain there, together with all the others he could never get rid of. He thought of the wooden-soled sandals on the slope and of his own child, as yet unborn; of how this child would look in nine years' time; of the horror and disgust that this crime would arouse, and what the front pages of the evening papers would look like.

The entire area around the gloomy, fortress-like water tower was roped off now, as well as the steep slope behind it, right down to the steps leading to Ingemarsgatan. He walked past the cars, stopped at the cordon and looked out over the empty playground with its sandpits and swings.

The knowledge that all this had happened before and was certain to happen again was a crushing burden. Since the last time they had got computers and more men and more cars. Since the last time the lighting in the parks had been improved and most of the bushes had been cleared away. Next time there would be still more cars and computers and even less shrubbery. Kollberg wiped his brow at the thought and the handkerchief was wet through.

The journalists and photographers were already there, but fortunately only a few of the inquisitive had as yet found their way here. The journalists and photographers, oddly enough, had become better with the years, partly thanks to the police. The inquisitive would never be any better.

The area around the water tower was strangely quiet, despite all the people. From afar, perhaps from the swimming pool or the playground at Sveavägen, cheerful shouts could be heard and children laughing.

Kollberg remained standing by the cordon. He said nothing, nor did anyone speak to him.

He knew that the homicide squad had been alerted, that the search was being stabilized, that men from the technical division were examining the scene of the crime, that the vice squad had been called in, that a central office was being organized to receive tips from the public, that a special inquiry squad was being prepared to go from door to door, that the coroner was ready and waiting, that every radio patrol car was on the watch, and that no resources would be spared, even his own.

Yet he allowed himself this moment of reflection. It was summer. People were swimming. Tourists were wandering about, map in hand. And in the shrubbery between the rocks and the red fence lay a dead child. It was horrible. And it might get worse.

Still another car, perhaps the ninth or tenth, hummed up the hill from Stefan's Church and stopped. Without actually turning his head, Kollberg saw Gunvald Larsson get out and come up to him.

'How is it going?'

'Don't know.'

'The rain. It poured with rain all night. Probably ...'

For once, Gunvald Larsson interrupted himself. After a moment he went on:

'If they take any footprints they're probably mine. I was here last evening. Soon after ten.'

'Oh.'

'The mugger. He struck down an old lady. Not fifty yards from here.'

'So I heard.'

'She had just shut up her fruit and confectionery kiosk and was on her way home. With the entire day's takings in her handbag.'

'Oh?'

'Every single penny of it. People are crazy,' Gunvald Larsson said.

He paused again. Nodded towards the rocks and the shrubbery and the red fence and said:

'She must have been lying there then.'

'Presumably.'

'It had already started raining when we got here. And the civil patrol, ninth district, had been here three quarters of an hour before the robbery. They didn't see anything either. She must have been lying here then too.'

'They were looking for the mugger,' Kollberg said.

'Yes. And when he got here they were in Lill-Jans Wood. This was the ninth time.'

'What about the old woman?'

'Ambulance case. Rushed to hospital. Shock, fractured jaw, four teeth knocked out, broken nose. All she saw of the man was that he had a red bandanna handkerchief over his face. Lousy description.'

Gunvald Larsson paused again and then said:

'If I'd had the dog van ...'

'What?'

'Your admirable pal Beck said that I should send out the dog van, when he was up last week. Maybe a dog would have found ...'

He nodded again in the direction of the rocks, as though unwilling to put what he meant into words.

Kollberg didn't like Gunvald Larsson particularly, but this time he sympathized with him.

'It's possible,' Kollberg said.

'Is it sex?' Gunvald Larsson asked with some hesitation.

'Presumably.'

'In that case I don't suppose there's any connection.'

'No, I don't suppose there is.'

Rönn came up to them from inside the cordon and Larsson said at once:

'Is it sex?'

'Yes,' Rönn said. 'Looks like it. Pretty certain.'

'Then there's no connection.'

'What with?'

'The mugger.'

'How are things going?' Kollberg asked.

'Badly,' Rönn said. 'Everything must have been washed away by the rain. She's soaked to the skin.'

'Christ, it's sickening,' Larsson said. 'Two maniacs prowling around the same place at the same time, one worse than the other.'

He turned on his heel and went back to the car. The last they heard him say was:

'Christ, what a bloody awful job. Who'd be a cop . . .'

Rönn watched him for a moment. Then he turned to Kollberg and said:

'Would you mind coming for a moment, sir?'

Kollberg sighed heavily and swung his legs over the rope.

Martin Beck did not go back to Stockholm until Saturday afternoon, the day before he was due back on duty. Ahlberg saw him off at the station.

He changed trains at Hallsberg and bought the evening papers at the station bookstall. Folded them and tucked them into his raincoat pocket and didn't open them until he had settled down on the express from Gothenburg.

He glanced at the banner headlines and gave a start. The nightmare had begun.

A few hours later for him than for the others. But that was about all.

9

There are moments and situations that one would like to avoid at all costs but which cannot be put off. Police are probably faced with such situations more often than other people, and without a doubt they occur more often for some policemen than for others.

One of these situations is to question a woman called Karin Carlsson less than twenty-four hours after she has learned that her eight-year-old daughter has been strangled by a sex maniac. A lone woman who, despite injections and pills, is still suffering from shock and is so apathetic that she is still wearing the same brown cotton housecoat and the same sandals she had on when a corpulent policeman she had never seen before and would never see again had rung her doorbell the day before. Moments such as that immediately before the questioning begins.

A detective superintendent in the homicide squad knows that this questioning cannot be put off, still less avoided, because apart from this one witness there is not a single clue to go on. Because there is not yet a report on the autopsy and because the contents of that report are more or less already known.

Twenty-four hours earlier Martin Beck had been sitting in the stern of a rowboat taking up the nets that he and Ahlberg had put down early the same morning. Now he was standing in a room at investigation headquarters at Kungsholmsgatan with his right elbow propped on a filing cabinet, far too ill at ease even to sit down.

It had been thought suitable for this questioning to be conducted by a woman, a detective inspector of the vice squad. She was about forty-five and her name was Sylvia Granberg. In some ways the choice was a very good one. Sitting at the desk opposite the woman in the brown housecoat she looked as unmoved as the tape recorder she had just started.

When she switched off the apparatus forty minutes later she had undergone no apparent change, nor had she once faltered. Martin Beck noticed this again when, a little later, he played back the tape together with Kollberg and a couple of others.

GRANBERG: I know it's hard for you, Mrs Carlsson, but unfortunately there are certain questions we must put to you.
WITNESS: Yes.
G: Your name is Karin Elisabet Carlsson?
W: Yes.
G: When were you born?
W: Sev . . . nineteenthir . . .
G: Can you try and keep your head turned towards the microphone when you answer?
W: Seventh of April 1937.
G: And your civil status?
W: What . . . I . . .
G: I mean are you single, married or divorced?
W: Divorced.
G: Since when?
W: Six years. Nearly seven.
G: And what is your ex-husband's name?
W: Sigvard Erik Bertil Carlsson.
G: Where does he live?

41

W: In Malmö . . . I mean he's registered there . . . I think.

G: Think? Don't you know?

MARTIN BECK: He's a seaman. We haven't been able to locate him yet.

G: Wasn't the husband liable for support of his daughter?

MB: Yes, of course, but he doesn't seem to have paid up for several years.

W: He . . . never really cared for Eva.

G: And your daughter's name was Eva Carlsson? No other first name?

W: No.

G: And she was born on the fifth of February 1959?

W: Yes.

G: Would you be good enough to tell us as exactly as possible what happened on Friday evening?

W: Happened . . . nothing happened. Eva . . . went out.

G: At what time?

W: Soon after seven. She'd been watching TV and we'd had our dinner.

G: What time was that?

W: At six o'clock. We always had dinner at six, when I got home. I work at a factory that makes lampshades . . . and I call for Eva at the afternoon nursery on the way home. She goes there herself after school . . . then we do the shopping on our way . . .

G: What did she have for dinner?

W: Meatballs . . . could I have a little water?

G: Of course. Here you are.

W: Thank you. Meatballs and mashed potatoes. And we had ice cream afterwards.

G: What did she drink?

W: Milk.

G: What did you do then?

W: We watched TV for a while . . . it was a children's programme.

G: And at seven o'clock or just after she went out?

W: Yes, it had stopped raining then. And the news had started on TV. She's not very interested in the news.

G: Did she go out alone?

W: Yes. Do you . . . you see it was quite light and the school holidays had begun. I told her she could stay out and play until eight. Do you think it . . . was careless of me?

G: Certainly not. By no means. Then you didn't see her again?

W: No . . . not until . . . no, I can't . . .

G: The identification? We needn't talk about that. When did you start getting worried?

W: I don't know. I was worried the whole time. I'm always worried when she's not at home. You see, she's all . . .

G: But when did you start looking for her?

W: Not until after half past eight. She's careless sometimes. Stays late with a playmate and forgets to look at the time. You know, children playing . . .

G: Yes. I see. When did you start searching?

W: About a quarter to nine. I knew she had two playmates the same age she used to go to. I called up the parents of one of them but got no answer.

MB: The family's away. Gone out to their summer cottage over the weekend.

W: I didn't know that. I don't think Eva did either.

G: What did you do then?

W: The other girl's parents have no telephone. So I went there.

G: What time?

W: I can't have got there until after nine, because the street door was locked and it took a while before I got in. I had to stand and wait until someone came. Eva had been there just after seven, but the other girl hadn't been allowed out. Her father said he thought it was too late for little girls to be out alone at that hour. (Pause)

W: Dear God if only I'd . . . But it was broad daylight and there were people everywhere. If only I hadn't . . .

G: Had your daughter left there at once?

w: Yes, she said she'd go to the playground.

G: Which playground do you think she meant?

w: The one in Vanadis Park, at Sveavägen. She always went there.

G: She can't have meant the other playground, the one up by the water tower?

w: I don't think so. She never went there. And certainly not alone.

G: Do you think she might have met some other playmates?

w: None that I know of. She always used to play with those two.

G: Well, when you didn't find her at this other place, what did you do then?

w: I . . . I went to the playground at Sveavägen. It was empty.

G: And then?

w: I didn't know what to do. I went home and waited. I stood in the window watching for her.

G: When did you call the police?

w: Not until later. At five or ten past ten I saw a police car stop by the park and then an ambulance came. It had started raining again by then. I put on my coat and ran there. I . . . I spoke to a policeman standing there, but he said it was an elderly woman who had hurt herself.

G: Did you go home again after that?

w: Yes. And I saw the light was on in the flat. I was so happy because I thought she had come home. But it was myself who had forgotten to put it out.

G: At what time did you call the police?

w: By half past ten I couldn't stand it any longer. I called up a friend, a woman I know at work. She lives at Hökarängen. She told me to call the police at once.

G: According to the information we have you called at ten minutes to eleven.

w: Yes. And then I went to the police station. The one in Surbrunnsgatan. They were awfully nice and kind. They asked me to tell them what Eva looks . . . looked like and what she had on. And I'd taken a snapshot with me so they could see what she looked like. They were so kind. The policeman who wrote everything down said that a lot of children got lost or stayed too long at the home of some playmate but that they all usually turned up safely after an hour or two. And ...

G: Yes?

W: And he said that if anything had happened, an accident or something, they'd have known about it by that time.

G: What time did you get home again?

W: It was after twelve by then. I sat up waiting ... all night. I waited for someone to ring. The police. They had my telephone number, you see, but no one called. I called them up once more anyway. But the man who answered said he had my number written down and that he'd call up at once if ... (Pause)

W: But no one called. No one at all. Not in the morning either. And then a plainclothes policeman came and ... and said ... said that ...

G: I don't think we need go on with this.

W: Oh, I see. No.

MB: Your daughter has been accosted by so-called molesters once or twice before, hasn't she?

W: Yes, last autumn. Twice. She thought she knew who it was. Someone who lived in the same block as Eivor, that's the friend who has no telephone.

MB: The one who lives in Hagagatan?

W: Yes. I reported it to the police. We were up here, in this building, and they got Eva to tell a lady all about it. They gave her a whole lot of pictures to look at too, in a big album.

G: There's a record of all that. We got the material out of the files.

MB: I know. But what I was going to ask is whether Eva was molested by this man later. After you reported him to the police?

W: No ... not as far as I know. She didn't say anything ... and she always tells me ...

G: Well, that's about all, Mrs Carlsson.

W: Oh. I see.

MB: Forgive my asking, but where are you going now?

W: I don't know. Not home to . . .

G: I'll come down with you and we can talk about it. We'll think of something.

W: Thank you. You're very kind.

Kollberg switched off the tape recorder, stared gloomily at Martin Beck and said:

'That bastard who molested her last autumn . . .'

'Yes?'

'It's the same one Rönn's busy with downstairs. We went and fetched him straight off at midday yesterday.'

'And?'

'So far it's merely a triumph for computer technique. He only grins and says it wasn't him.'

'Which proves?'

'Nothing, of course. He has no alibi either. Says he was at home asleep in his one-room flat at Hagagatan. Can't quite remember, he says.'

'Can't remember?'

'He's a complete alcoholic,' Kollberg said. 'At any rate we know that he sat drinking at the Röda Berget restaurant until he was chucked out at about six o'clock. It doesn't look too good for him.'

'What did he do last time?'

'Exposed himself. He's an ordinary exhibitionist, as far as I can make out. I have the tape of the interview with the girl here. Yet another triumph for technology.'

The door opened and Rönn came in.

'Well?' Kollberg asked.

'Nothing so far. We'll have to let him come round a bit. Seems done in.'

'So do you,' Kollberg said.

He was right; Rönn looked unnaturally pale and his eyes were swollen and red-rimmed.

'What do you think?' Martin Beck asked.

'I don't know what to think,' Rönn replied. 'I think I'm sickening for something.'

'You can do that later,' Kollberg said. 'Not now. Let's listen to this tape.'

Martin Beck nodded. The spool of the recorder started turning again. A pleasant female voice said:

'Questioning of schoolgirl Eva Carlsson born fifth of February 1959. Examining officer Detective Inspector Sonja Hansson.'

Both Martin Beck and Kollberg frowned and missed the next few sentences. They recognized the name and voice all too well. Sonja Hansson was a girl whose death they had very nearly brought about two and a half years earlier when they used her as decoy in a police trap.

'A miracle she stayed on in the force,' Kollberg said.

'Yes,' Martin Beck agreed.

'Quiet, I can't hear,' Rönn said.

He had not been mixed up in it that time.

'. . . so then this man came up to you?'

'Yes. Eivor and I were standing at the bus stop.'

'What did he do?'

'He smelled nasty and he had a funny walk, and he said . . . it was so funny what he said.'

'Can you remember what it was?'

'Yes, he said, "Hello, little girlies, will you jerk me off if I give you five kronor?"'

'Do you know what he meant by that, Eva?'

'No, it was so funny. I know what jerk is, because sometimes the girl sitting next to me at school jerks my elbow. But why did the man want us to jerk his elbow? He wasn't sitting down and writing or anything, and anyway . . .'

'What did you do then? After he had said that?'

'He said it several times. Then he walked off and we crept after him.'

'Crept after him?'

'Yes, shadowed him. Like on the movies or TV.'

'Did you dare to?'

'Humph, there was no harm in it.'

'Oh yes, Eva, you should watch out for men like that.'

'Humph, he wasn't dangerous.'

'Did you see which way he went?'

'Yes, he went into the flats where Eivor lives and two floors above hers he took out a key and went inside.'

'Did you both go home then?'

'Oh no. We crept up and looked at the door. It had his name on it, see.'

'Yes, I see. And what was his name?'

'Eriksson, I think. We listened through the letter box too. We could hear him mumbling.'

'Did you tell your mother about it?'

'Humph, it was nothing. But it *was* funny.'

'But you did tell your mother about what happened yesterday?'

'About the cows, yes.'

'Was it the same man?'

'Ye-es.'

'Are you sure?'

'Almost.'

'How old do you think this man is?'

'Oh, about twenty at least.'

'How old do you think I am?'

'Oh, about forty. Or fifty.'

'Is this man older or younger than I am, do you think?'

'Oh, much older. Much, much older. How old are you?'

'Twenty-eight. Well, can you tell me what happened yesterday?'

'Well, Eivor and I were playing hopscotch in the doorway and he came up and stood there and said, "Come along with me, girlies, and you can watch me milking my cows."'

'I see. And what did he do then?'

'Humph, he couldn't have cows up in his room. Not real ones.'

'What did you say, you and Eivor?'

'Oh, we didn't say anything, but afterwards Eivor said she was ashamed because her hair ribbon had come undone so she wasn't going home with *anybody*.'

'Did the man go home then?'

'No, he said, "Well, I'll just have to milk my cows here then." Then he undid his trousers and . . .'

'Yes?'

'I say, do you think that if Eivor's hair ribbon hadn't come undone, we might have been murdered? How exciting . . .'

'No, I don't think so. The man undid his trousers, you said?'

'Yes, and then he took out that thing that men do wee-wee with . . .'

The clear childish voice was cut off in the middle of the sentence as Kollberg reached out and switched off the tape recorder. Martin Beck looked at him. Propped his head on his left hand and rubbed his nose with his knuckles.

'The funny thing about this is . . .' Rönn began.

'What the hell are you saying,' Kollberg barked.

'Well, he admits it now. The time before, he swore blind he didn't, and the girls got more and more uncertain about identifying him, so nothing came of it. But now he confesses. Says he was drunk both times, else he wouldn't have done it.'

'Oh, so he admits it now,' Kollberg said.

'Yes.'

Martin Beck glanced inquiringly at Kollberg. Then he turned to Rönn and said:

'You didn't get any sleep last night, did you?'

'No.'

'Then you'd better go home and catch up on it.'

'Shall we let this fellow go?'

'No,' Kollberg said. 'We won't let him go.'

49

10

Sure enough, the man's name was Eriksson. He was a warehouseman and it didn't take an expert to see that he was an alcoholic. He was sixty years old, tall, bald and emaciated. His whole body twitched and shook.

Kollberg and Martin Beck questioned him for two hours, which were equally wretched for all concerned.

The man admitted the same disgusting details over and over again. At intervals he sniffled and sobbed, calling heaven to witness that he had gone straight home from the restaurant on Friday afternoon. At any rate he couldn't remember anything else.

After two hours he confessed that he had stolen two hundred kronor in July 1964 and a cycle when he was eighteen. He then did nothing but snivel. He was a human wreck, an outcast from the dubious fellowship that surrounded him, and utterly alone.

Kollberg and Martin Beck regarded him gloomily and sent him back to the cell.

At the same time other men from the division, and from the fifth district, tried to find someone in the flats at Hagagatan who could either confirm or confute his alibi. They were not successful.

* * *

The autopsy report available about four o'clock that afternoon was still preliminary. It spoke of strangulation, finger marks on the neck and sexual assault. Out-and-out rape had not been established.

Otherwise the report contained negative information. There was no indication that the girl had had a chance to resist. No scrapings of skin had been found under the nails and no bruises on arms and hands, though there were some on the lower abdomen, as if caused by blows of a fist.

The technical division had examined her clothes, and had nothing unusual to report. Her panties, however, were missing. They couldn't be found anywhere. They had been white cotton, size 6, and a well-known make.

In the evening the men detailed to go around from door to door had handed out five hundred stencilled questionnaires. Only one reply of any interest had been received. An eighteen-year-old girl by the name of Majken Jansson, who lived in the apartment building at Sveavägen 103 and was the daughter of a businessman, said that she and a boyfriend her own age had spent about twenty minutes in Vanadis Park some time between eight and nine. She wasn't sure of the exact time. They had seen nothing and heard nothing.

Asked what they had been doing in Vanadis Park, she had replied that they had been at a family dinner party and had just gone out to get a breath of air.

'A breath of air,' Melander said thoughtfully.

'Between the legs, no doubt,' Gunvald Larsson said.

Larsson had been in the regular navy and was still in the reserve. Now and then he gave vent to his below-decks humour.

Hour after hour dragged past. The investigation machinery went grinding on. The time was already past one o'clock on the night between Sunday and Monday when Martin Beck came home to Bagarmossen. Everyone was asleep. He took a can of beer out of the fridge and made a cheese sandwich. Then he drank the beer and threw the sandwich into the bin.

After he had got into bed he lay for a while thinking of the alcoholic warehouseman called Eriksson, who three years ago had stolen two hundred kronor from a workmate's coat.

Kollberg couldn't get to sleep. He lay in the dark staring at the ceiling. He too thought of the man called Eriksson whose name had been in the vice squad's register. He also considered the fact that if the man who had committed the murder in Vanadis Park was not in the register, then computer technology was about as much good to them as it had been to the American police in their hunt for the Boston strangler. In other words, none at all. The Boston strangler had killed thirteen people, all lone women, in two years without leaving a single clue.

Now and then he looked at his wife. She was asleep, but twitched every time the baby in her body kicked.

11

It was Monday afternoon, fifty-four hours after the dead girl had been found in Vanadis Park.

The police had appealed to the public for help through the press, radio and television, and over three hundred tips had already come in. Each item of information was registered and examined by a special working group, after which the results were studied in detail.

The vice squad combed its registers, the forensic laboratory dealt with the meagre material from the scene of the crime, the computers worked at high pressure, men from the assault squad went around the neighbourhood knocking on doors, suspects and possible witnesses were questioned, and as yet all this activity had led nowhere. The murderer was unknown and still at large.

The papers were piling up on Martin Beck's desk. Since early morning he had been working on the never-ceasing stream of reports and interrogation statements. The telephone had never stopped ringing, but in order to get a breathing space he had now asked Kollberg to take his calls during the next hour or so. Gunvald Larsson and Melander were spared all these telephone calls; they sat behind closed doors sifting material.

Martin Beck had had only a few hours' sleep during the night and he had skipped lunch so as to have time for a press conference, which had yielded the journalists very little.

He yawned and looked at the time, astonished that it was already a quarter past three. Gathering up a bundle of papers that belonged to Melander's department, he knocked at the door and went in to Melander and Larsson.

Melander did not look up when he entered the room. They had worked together for so long that he knew Martin Beck's knock. Gunvald Larsson glared at the bundle of papers in Martin Beck's hand and said:

'Good God, have you brought still more? We're swamped with work already.'

Martin Beck shrugged and put the papers down at Melander's elbow.

'I was going to order some coffee,' he said. 'Like some?'

Melander shook his head without looking up.

'Good idea,' Gunvald Larsson said.

Martin Beck went out, shut the door behind him and collided with Kollberg, who had come rushing up. Martin Beck saw the frantic expression on Kollberg's round face and asked:

'What's up with you?'

Kollberg gripped his arm and said, so fast that the words tumbled over each other:

'Martin, it has happened again! He has done it again! In Tanto Park.'

They drove across the West Bridge with sirens full on, and on the radio they heard that all available patrol cars had been directed to Tanto Park to cordon it off. All that Martin Beck and Kollberg had been told before leaving headquarters was that a girl had been found dead near the open-air theatre, that the circumstances were similar to the murder in Vanadis Park and that the body had been found so soon after the crime that there was a chance the murderer had not yet got very far.

As they drove past the Zinkensdamm athletic field they saw a couple of black-and-white cars turn into Wollmar Yxkullsgatan. One or two more were standing in Ringvägen and inside the park.

They pulled up outside the row of old wooden houses in Sköldgatan. The road into the park was blocked by a car with a radio aerial. On the footpath they saw a uniformed police officer stop some children who were on their way up the hill.

Martin Beck strode swiftly towards the officer, leaving Kollberg to follow as best he could. The policeman saluted and pointed up into the park. Martin Beck strode on without slackening his pace. The park was very hummocky and not until he had passed the theatre and climbed the slope did he see some men standing in a semicircle with their backs to him. They were in a hollow about thirty yards from the road. Farther away, where the road forked, a uniformed policeman was on guard to keep inquisitive people away.

As he went down the slope Kollberg caught up with him. They could hear the policemen down there talking, but they fell silent as Beck and Kollberg approached. The men saluted and stepped aside. Martin Beck heard Kollberg panting.

The girl was lying on her back in the grass with both arms bent over her head. The left leg was bent and the knee drawn up so high to the side that the thigh lay at right angles to the body. The right leg lay stretched out obliquely from the trunk. Her face was turned upwards, with half-closed eyes and open mouth. Blood had trickled down from the nostrils. A skipping rope of yellow transparent plastic was wound tightly around her neck in several coils. She was wearing a yellow sleeveless cotton dress buttoned right down the front. The three bottom buttons had been torn off. She had no panties. On her feet were white socks and red sandals. She looked about ten years old. She was dead.

Martin Beck saw all this during the few seconds he was able to keep his eyes on her. Then he turned and looked towards the road. Two of the men from the technical division were running down the slope. They were dressed in grey-blue coveralls and one of them was carrying a large grey metal box. The second man had a coil of rope in one hand and a black bag in the other. As they got nearer the man with the rope called:

'That bastard who has left his car in the middle of the road will have to move it so that we can drive up.'

Then, glancing at the dead girl, he ran down to the road fork and began cordoning off the area with the rope.

A radio policeman in a leather jacket was standing beside the road speaking into a walkie-talkie while a plainclothes man stood beside him listening. Martin Beck recognized the plainclothes man. His name was Manning and he belonged to the protection squad in second district.

Manning caught sight of Martin Beck and Kollberg, said a few words to the radio policeman and then came up to them.

'It seems as if the whole area is cordoned off now,' he said. 'As far as possible.'

'How long since she was found?' Martin Beck asked.

Manning looked at his wrist watch.

'It's twenty-five minutes since the first car got here,' he said.

'And you've no description to go on?' Kollberg asked.

'No, unfortunately.'

'Who found her?' Martin Beck asked.

'A couple of small boys. They gave the alarm to a radio car that was driving along Ringvägen. She was still warm when they got here. Doesn't seem to be long since it happened.'

Martin Beck looked around him. The technical division car was driving down the slope, closely followed by the doctor's.

From the hollow where the dead child's body lay nothing could be seen of the allotment gardens that began behind a mound about fifty yards to the west. Above the treetops the upper storeys of one of the blocks of flats in Tantogatan were visible, but the railway line that divided the street from the park was hidden by the greenery.

'He couldn't have chosen a better spot in the whole of Stockholm,' Martin Beck said.

'A worse one, you mean,' Kollberg said.

He was right. Even if the man guilty of the little girl's death was still within the area, he had a pretty good chance of escaping. The park is the biggest in the inner part of the city. Next to Tanto Park itself there are allotment gardens and cottages, and below them, on the shore of Årstaviken, is a straggling line of small boatyards, storehouses, workshops, scrapyards and ramshackle wooden huts. Between Wollmar Yxkullsgatan, which cuts through the area from Ringvägen to the water, and Hornsgatan lies the Högalid Institution for alcoholics, consisting of several large, irregularly placed buildings. Round about are several more storehouses and wooden sheds. Between the institution and the Zinkensdamm athletic ground is yet another colony of allotment gardens. A viaduct over the railway connects the south side of the park with Tantogatan, where five gigantic blocks of flats have been built on the rocks nearest the water. Farther up, at the corner of Ringvägen, is the Tanto workingmen's hostel, consisting of a line of low, sprawling wooden huts.

Martin Beck sized up the situation as almost hopeless. He did not see how they could possibly catch the murderer here and now. For one thing, they didn't even have his description; for another, he was sure to have made a clear getaway by this time. Thirdly, the alcoholics' home and the workingmen's hostel could supply them with so many suspicious individuals that it would take days to question them.

The next hour confirmed his doubts. When the doctor had finished his preliminary examination he could merely say that the girl had been strangled and probably raped, and that death had occurred quite recently. The dog van had arrived soon after Martin Beck and Kollberg, but the only scent the dogs picked up led straight out of the park towards Wollmar Yxkullsgatan. The plainclothes policemen in the protection squad were questioning possible witnesses, as yet without result. A number of people had been in the park and the allotment gardens, but no one had seen or heard anything that could be connected with the murder.

The time was ten minutes to five and on Ringvägen a group of people stood on the pavement staring inquisitively at the apparently aimless work of the police. Reporters and photographers had arrived in a stream; some of them had already returned to their editorial offices to supply readers with juicy descriptions of the second murder of a little girl in Stockholm within the space of three days, committed by a maniac who was still at large.

Martin Beck caught sight of Kollberg's round behind in the open door of a radio car that was parked on the gravel nearest Ringvägen. He broke away from a cluster of journalists and went up to Kollberg, who was leaning into the car and speaking on the radio. He waited until Kollberg had finished speaking and then pinched his behind. Kollberg backed out of the car and straightened up.

'Oh, it's you. I thought it was one of the dogs.'

'Do you know if anyone has told the girl's parents?' Martin Beck asked.

'Yes,' Kollberg replied. 'We're spared that.'

'I thought I'd go and talk to the boys who found her. They live over there in Tantogatan.'

'Okay,' Kollberg said. 'I'll stay here.'

'Fine. Be seeing you,' Martin Beck said.

The boys lived in one of the big bow-shaped apartment blocks in Tantogatan and Martin Beck found them both at home. They were suffering from shock after their awful experience, but at the same time could not hide the fact that they found it all very exciting.

They told Martin Beck how they had stumbled on the girl while playing in the park. They had recognized her at once, as she lived in the same block as they did. Earlier in the day they had seen her in the playground behind the flats where they lived. She had been skipping together with two girls of her own age. As one of them was in the same class as the boys, they could tell Martin Beck that her name was Lena Oskarsson, that she was ten years old and lived next door.

The next block of flats looked exactly like the one the boys lived in. He took the swift automatic lift to the seventh floor and rang the doorbell. After a while the door was opened and then shut again immediately. He had not seen anyone through the crack of the door. He rang the bell a second time. The door was opened at once and he now realized why he had not seen anyone the first time. The boy standing inside looked about three years old and his flaxen-coloured head was about a yard below the level of Martin Beck's eyes.

The lad let go of the door handle and said in a high-pitched, clear voice:

'Hi, good afternoon.'

Then he ran into the flat and Martin Beck heard him call:

'Mummy! Mummy! Big man come.'

About half a minute passed before his mother came to the door. She looked anxiously and questioningly at Martin Beck and he hastened to show his badge.

'I'd like a word with your daughter if she's at home,' he said. 'Does she know what has happened?'

'To Annika? Yes, we heard just now from a neighbour. It's horrible. How can such a thing happen in broad daylight? But come in. I'll get Lena.'

Martin Beck followed Mrs Oskarsson into the living room. Apart from the furniture, it was identical with the room he had just left. The little boy was standing in the middle of the floor, looking at him with expectant curiosity. He was holding a toy guitar.

'Go into your room and play, Bosse,' his mother said.

Bosse took no notice, and she didn't seem to expect him to.

She went over and moved some toys off the sofa by the balcony window.

'It's rather untidy here,' she said. 'Won't you sit down, and I'll get Lena.'

She left the room and Martin Beck smiled at the little boy. His own children were twelve and fifteen and he had forgotten how to make conversation with three-year-olds.

'Can you play that guitar?' he asked.

'Not lay,' the boy said. 'You lay.'

'No, I can't play.'

'Yes, you lay,' the boy persisted.

Mrs Oskarsson came in, picked up the boy and the guitar and carried him firmly out of the room. He screamed and kicked and his mother said over her shoulder:

'I'll be back in a minute. You can be talking to Lena.'

The boys had said that Lena was ten years old. She was tall for her age and rather pretty, despite a slight pout. She was dressed in jeans and a cotton shirt and she bobbed shyly.

'Sit down,' Martin Beck said. 'We can talk better then.'

She sat on the edge of one of the armchairs with her knees pressed together.

'Your name's Lena, isn't it?' he said.

'Yes.'

'And mine's Martin. You know what has happened?'

'Yes,' the girl said, staring at the floor. 'I heard . . . Mum told me.'

'I know you must be upset, but I have to ask you one or two things.'

'Yes.'

'You were together with Annika earlier today, weren't you?'

'Yes, we played together. Ulla and Annika and I.'

'Where did you play?'

She nodded towards the window.

'First in the yard down here. Then Ulla had to go home for

60

lunch, so Annika and I came home here. Then Ulla called for us and we went out again.'

'Where to?'

'To Tanto Park. I had to take Bosse with me and there are swings there and he likes that.'

'Do you know what the time was then?'

'Oh, half past one, getting on for two maybe. Mum might know.'

'So then you went to Tanto Park. Did you see if Annika met anyone there? If a man spoke to her or anything?'

'No, I didn't see her talking to anyone.'

'What did you do in Tanto Park?'

The girl stared out of the window for a while. She seemed to be thinking back.

'Let me see . . . we played. First we were on the swings because Bosse wanted it. Then we did some skipping. Then we went down to the stand and bought an ice cream.'

'Were there any other children in the park?'

'Not just where we were. Oh yes, there were some small children in the sandpit. Bosse went and pestered them. But they went away after a while with their mother.'

'What did you do when you'd bought the ice cream?' Martin Beck asked.

From another room he heard Mrs Oskarsson's voice and the boy's scream of rage.

'We just walked about. Then Annika got the sulks.'

'Got the sulks? Why?'

'Oh, she just did. Ulla and I wanted to play hopscotch, but she didn't. She wanted to play hide-and-seek, but it's no good when Bosse's there. He runs about telling everyone where you've hidden. So she got cross and went off.'

'Where to? Did she say where she was going?'

'No, she didn't say. She just went off, and Ulla and I were drawing the squares for the hopscotch so we didn't see when she left.'

'You didn't see which way she went?'

'No, we never gave it a thought. We played hopscotch and after a while I noticed that Bosse had disappeared and then we saw that Annika had gone too.'

'Did you go and look for Bosse?'

The girl looked down at her hands and it was some moments before she answered.

'No. I thought he was with Annika. He's always running after Annika. She has . . . she had no small brothers or sisters of her own and was awfully nice to Bosse, always.'

'What happened then? Did Bosse come back?'

'Yes, after a while he came back. I suppose he'd been somewhere close by although we didn't see him.'

Martin Beck nodded. He wanted to light a cigarette but saw no ashtrays in the room and refrained.

'Where do you think Annika was then? Did Bosse say anything about where he had gone?'

The girl shook her head and a lock of fair hair fell down over her forehead.

'No, we just thought she'd gone home. We didn't ask Bosse and he said nothing. Then he got so naughty that we came home.'

'Do you know what the time was when Annika disappeared from the playground?'

'No, I had no watch. But it was three o'clock when we got home. And we didn't play hopscotch for long. Half an hour or so.'

'Didn't you see anyone else in the park?'

Lena pushed back her hair and frowned.

'We never thought about it. At any rate I didn't. Yes, there was a lady there with her dog for a while. A dachshund. Bosse wanted to pat it so I had to go and get him.'

She looked gravely at Martin Beck.

'He's not to pat dogs, it's dangerous.'

'You didn't notice anyone else in the park? Think back now, perhaps you can remember someone?'

She shook her head.

'No. We were playing and I had to keep an eye on Bosse, so I never thought about who was in the park. I suppose some people walked past, but I don't know.'

There was silence now in the room next door and Mrs Oskarsson came back. Martin Beck got up.

'Would you mind giving me Ulla's name and address?' he said to the girl. 'Then I'll go, but I may have to talk to you again. If you happen to think of anything that happened or anything you saw in the park, will you ask your mother to call me?'

He turned to Mrs Oskarsson.

'It might be some detail that seems unimportant,' he said. 'But I'd be glad if you'd call me in case she remembers anything more.'

He gave her his card, and she wrote down the third girl's name, address and telephone number on a slip of paper and handed it to him.

Then he went back to Tanto Park.

The men from the technical division were still working in the hollow below the open-air theatre. The sun was low in the sky and cast long shadows across the grass. Martin Beck stayed until the dead girl had been taken away. Then he drove back to police headquarters at Kungsholmsgatan.

'And he took the girl's panties with him this time too,' Gunvald Larsson said.

'Yes,' Martin Beck said. 'White. Size 6.'

'The bastard,' Larsson said.

Poking at his ear with a pen he said:

'And what did your four-legged friends think of the case?'

Martin Beck looked at him with disapproval.

'What are we to do with this man Eriksson?' Rönn asked.

'Let him go,' Martin Beck said.

After a few seconds he added:

'But not too far.'

12

On the morning of Tuesday 13 June the situation was reviewed; the results of the investigation so far were anything but hopeful. The same could be said of the short statement released to the press. The areas around the scenes of the two crimes had been photographed from a helicopter; about a thousand tips had been received from the public and were now being followed up; all exhibitionists, Peeping Toms and other sexual deviates known to the police were being checked up on; one individual had been detained and questioned about his doings at the time of the first crime; this person had now been set free.

Everyone seemed worn out from lack of sleep and overwork, even the journalists and photographers.

After the review Kollberg said to Martin Beck:

'There are two witnesses.'

Martin Beck nodded. They both went into the office where Gunvald Larsson and Melander were working.

'There are two witnesses,' Martin Beck said.

Melander didn't even look up from his papers but Larsson said:

'Hell, you don't say. And who would they be?'

'First, the boy in Tanto Park.'

'Who is three years old?'

'Exactly.'

'The girls in the vice squad have tried to talk to him, you know that as well as I do. He can't even talk. It's just about as clever as when you told me to question the dog.'

Martin Beck ignored both the remark and the astonished look that Kollberg gave him.

'And secondly?' Melander asked, still without looking up.

'The mugger.'

'He's my department,' Gunvald Larsson said.

'Exactly. Get him.'

Gunvald Larsson heaved himself back so that the swivel chair creaked. He stared from Martin Beck to Kollberg and said:

'Look here. What do you think I've been doing for three weeks, I and the protection squads of fifth and ninth? Playing Chinese chequers? Are you insinuating that we haven't tried?'

'You've tried all right. Now the position has changed. Now you must get him.'

'And how the hell are we to do that? Now?'

'The mugger knows his job,' Martin Beck said. 'You said so yourself. Has he at any time attacked anyone who didn't have money?'

'No.'

'Has he at any time gone for anyone who could defend himself?' Kollberg asked.

'No.'

'Have the boys in the protection squad ever been anywhere near?' Martin Beck asked.

'No.'

'And what can be the reason?' Kollberg asked again.

Gunvald Larsson did not answer at once. He poked his ear for a long time with the ball-point pen before saying:

'He knows his job.'

'That's what you said.'

Gunvald Larsson pondered again for a time. Then he asked:

'When you were up here ten days ago you started to say something but changed your mind. Why?'

'Because you interrupted me.'

'What were you going to say?'

'That we ought to study the timetable for the robberies,' Melander said, still without looking up. 'The systematics. We've already done so.'

'One more thing,' Martin Beck said. 'The same as Lennart here implied just now. The mugger is a skilled workman and knows his job, your own conclusion. He's so good at it that he recognizes the men in the protection squads. Perhaps even the cars.'

'So what?' Gunvald Larsson said. 'Do you mean we should change the whole damn police force just because of this louse?'

'You could have got in men from outside,' Kollberg said. 'Policewomen as well. Other cars.'

'It's too late now anyway,' Larsson said.

'Yes,' Martin Beck agreed. 'It's too late now. On the other hand it's twice as urgent for us to get him.'

'That guy's not even going to look at a park so long as the murderer goes free,' Gunvald Larsson said.

'Exactly. At what time was the last robbery committed?'

'Between nine and a quarter past.'

'And the murder?'

'Between seven and eight. Look here, why do you stand there asking about things we all know?'

'Sorry. Perhaps I wanted to convince myself.'

'What of?'

'Of the fact that the mugger saw the girl,' Kollberg said. 'And the man who killed her. The mugger wasn't the sort of guy to act haphazardly. Presumably he had to hang about the park for hours every time before he got his chance. Otherwise he had fantastic luck.'

'Such luck doesn't exist,' Melander said. 'Not nine times in succession. Five perhaps. Or six.'

'Get him,' Martin Beck said.

'Appeal to his sense of justice, eh? So that he gives himself up?'

'Even that is possible.'

'Yes,' Melander said, speaking on the phone.

He listened for a moment and said:

'Send a radio patrol.'

'Was it anything?' Kollberg asked.

'No,' Melander said.

'Sense of justice,' Gunvald Larsson said, shaking his head. 'Your naive faith in the underworld is really . . . humph, words fail me.'

'Just at the moment I don't give a damn what fails you,' Martin Beck said heatedly. 'Get that guy.'

'Use the snouts,' Kollberg said.

'Do you think I don't . . .' Gunvald Larsson began, but was himself interrupted for once.

'Wherever he is,' Martin Beck said. 'Whether he's in the Canary Islands or is lying low in a junkie's squat on the south side. Use the snouts, and do so much more than before. Use every single contact we have in the underworld, use the newspapers and the radio and the television. Threaten, bribe, coax, promise, do anything at all, but get that guy.'

'Do you think I haven't the sense to grasp that myself?'

'You know what I think of your intelligence,' Kollberg said gravely.

'Yes, I know,' Gunvald Larsson said good-naturedly. 'Well, let's clear the decks for action.'

He grabbed the telephone. Martin Beck and Kollberg left the room.

'Maybe it'll work,' Martin Beck said.

'Maybe,' Kollberg replied.

'Gunvald isn't as stupid as he looks.'

'Isn't he?'

'Er . . . Lennart.'

'Yes?'

'Just what's wrong with you?'

'The same as what's wrong with you.'

'And that is?'

'I'm scared.'

Martin Beck made no reply to this. Partly because Kollberg was right, partly because they had known each other for so long that words were not always necessary.

Impelled by the same thought they went downstairs and into the street. The car, a red Saab, had a provincial numberplate, but belonged nevertheless to the police headquarters in Stockholm.

'That little boy, whatever his name is,' Martin Beck said thoughtfully.

'Bo Oskarsson. Known as Bosse.'

'I met him just for a moment. Who was it that talked to him?'

'Sylvia, I think. Or maybe it was Sonja.'

The streets were fairly empty and the heat was oppressive. They drove over the West Bridge, turned down to the Pålsund Canal and continued along Bergsundsstrand, listening the whole time to the chatter of the radio patrols on the 40-metre waveband.

'Any damned radio ham within a radius of fifty miles can poke his nose into that,' Kollberg said irritably. 'Do you know what it would cost to screen off a private radio transmitter?'

Martin Beck nodded. He had heard that the cost was in the region of 150,000 kronor. Money that wasn't there.

Actually they were thinking of something quite different. Last time they had made an all-out effort to catch a murderer it had taken forty days before he was seized. The last time they had had a case like this it had taken about ten days. Now the murderer had struck twice within less than four days. Melander had said that the mugger might have been lucky five or six times. Quite feasible. Applied to the present case this was no longer mathematics but a vision of horror.

They drove under Liljeholm Bridge, along Hornstull Strand,

passed under the railway bridge and turned up into the residential area where the old sugar mill had once been. Some children were playing in the gardens around the flats, but not many.

They parked the car and took the lift to the seventh floor. Rang the doorbell, but no one came to the door. After waiting a while Martin Beck rang the bell of the flat next door. A woman opened the door a chink. Behind her he caught a glimpse of a little girl of five or six.

'The police,' Kollberg said reassuringly, showing his badge.

'Oh,' the woman said.

'Do you know if the Oskarsson family are at home?' Martin Beck asked.

'No, they went away this morning. To relations somewhere. That's to say the wife and children.'

'Oh, I'm sorry to have ...'

'But it's not everyone who can,' the woman cut in. 'I mean go away.'

'Do you know where they went?' Kollberg asked.

'No. But they'll be back on Friday morning. Then I think they're leaving again right away.'

She looked at them and said in explanation:

'Their holiday starts then.'

'But the husband is at home?'

'Yes, this evening. You can call him.'

'Yes,' Martin Beck said.

The little girl grew fretful and tugged at her mother's skirts.

'The children get so peevish,' she said. 'You can't let them out. Or is it all right?'

'Preferably not.'

'But some people have to,' the woman said. 'And a lot of children won't obey.'

'Yes, unfortunately.'

Without a word they went down in the lift. Without a word they drove northwards through the city, aware of their powerlessness and of their ambivalent attitude to the society they were there to protect.

They swung up into Vanadis Park and were stopped by a uniformed police officer who recognized neither them nor the car. There was nothing to see in the park. Except a few children who were playing, in spite of everything. And the indefatigable snoopers.

When they got back to the intersection of Odengatan and Sveavägen Kollberg said:

'I'm thirsty.'

Martin Beck nodded. They parked, went into the Metropole restaurant and ordered fruit juice.

Two other men were sitting at the bar. They had taken off their coats and put them on the bar stools, an act of unconventionalism that showed how hot it really was. They were drinking whisky and soda, and talking earnestly between sips.

'It's because there's no proper punishment,' the younger man said. 'A lynching is what's needed.'

'Yes,' the older man agreed.

'I'm sorry to have to say it, but it's the only thing.'

Kollberg opened his mouth to say something but changed his mind and drained his glass of fruit juice in one gulp.

Martin Beck was to hear much the same thing once more that day. In a tobacconist's, when he went in to buy a pack of cigarettes. The man in front of him was saying:

'. . . and do you know what they ought to do when they catch this bastard? They ought to execute him in public, they should show it on TV, and they shouldn't do it all at once. No, bit by bit for several days.'

When the man had gone Martin Beck said:

'Who was that?'

'His name's Skog,' the tobacconist said. 'He has the radio workshop next door. Decent chap.'

Back at headquarters Martin Beck reflected that it wasn't so long since they used to chop a thief's hands off. Yet people still went on stealing. Plenty of them.

In the evening he called up Bo Oskarsson's father.

'Ingrid and the children? I've sent them down to her mother and father in Öland. No, there's no phone there.'

'And when will they be back?'

'On Friday morning. The very same evening we're going abroad. We don't damn well dare to stay here.'

'No,' Martin Beck said wearily.

This was what happened on Tuesday 13 June.

On Wednesday nothing at all happened. The weather grew hotter.

13

Soon after eleven o'clock on Thursday something did happen. Martin Beck was standing in what had become his habitual position with his right elbow propped on the filing cabinet and heard the phone ring for what must have been the fiftieth time that morning. Gunvald Larsson answered:

'Larsson.

'What?

'Okay, I'll be down right away.'

He stood up and said to Martin Beck:

'It was the doorman. There's a girl down there who says she knows something.'

'About what?'

Larsson was already in the doorway.

'The mugger.'

A minute later the girl was sitting by the desk. She could not have been more than twenty but looked older. She was wearing purple net stockings, high-heeled shoes with open toes and a miniskirt. Her cleavage was remarkable, and so was the arrangement of her dyed hair; the eyelashes were false and the eyeshadow had been plastered on. Her mouth was small and pouting and her breasts stuck right up in the bra.

'What is it you know?' Gunvald Larsson said immediately.

'You wanted to know about him in Vasa Park and Vanadis Park and so on,' she said pertly. 'At any rate so I heard.'

'What else did you come here for?'

'Don't rush me,' she said with a toss of her head.

'What do you know?' Larsson said impatiently.

'I think you're being offensive,' she said. 'Funny the way all cops are so damn fresh.'

'If it's the reward you're after, there isn't one,' Larsson said.

'You can stuff your reward,' the lady said.

'Why have you come?' Martin Beck asked as gently as he could.

'I've got all the dosh I want,' she said.

Obviously she had come to make a scene – at least that was partly the reason – and was not going to be put off. Martin Beck could see the veins swelling on Gunvald Larsson's forehead. The girl said:

'Anyway, I earn a damn sight more than you do.'

'Yes, with your cu—,' Larsson said, but checked himself and went on:

'I think the less said the better about the way you earn your money.'

'One more word like that and I go,' she said.

'You're not going anywhere,' Larsson retorted.

'It's a free country, isn't it? A democracy or whatever it's called?'

'Why have you come here?' Martin Beck asked, only a fraction less gently than the time before.

'Yes, you really want to know, don't you? Your ears are flapping. I've a good mind to leave without saying a word.'

Melander was the one who broke the deadlock. He raised his head, took the pipe out of his mouth, looked at her for the first time since she had entered the room and said quietly:

'Won't you tell us, my dear?'

'About him in Vanadis Park and Vasa Park and . . .'

'Yes, if you really know something,' Melander said.

'And then I can go?'

'Of course.'

'Word of honour?'

'Word of honour,' Melander replied.

'And you won't tell him ...'

She shrugged, speaking mostly to herself:

'Humph, he'll guess anyway.'

'What's his name?' Melander said.

'Roffe.'

'And his surname?'

'Lundgren. Rolf Lundgren.'

'Where does he live?' Gunvald Larsson asked.

'Luntmakargatan 57.'

'And where is he now?'

'There,' she said.

'How do you know for sure he's the one?' Martin Beck asked.

He saw something glisten in the girl's eyes and realized with astonishment that it must be tears.

'As if I didn't know,' she mumbled.

'So you're going steady with this guy,' Larsson said.

She stared at him without answering.

'What's the name on the door?' Melander asked.

'Simonsson.'

'Whose flat is it?' Martin Beck asked.

'His. Roffe's. I think.'

'It doesn't add up,' Larsson said.

'I suppose he rents it on a sublet. Do you think he's fool enough to have his own name on the door?'

'Is he wanted?'

'I don't know.'

'On the run?'

'I don't know.'

'Oh yes, you do,' Martin Beck said. 'Has he broken out of prison?'

'No, he hasn't. Roffe has never been caught.'

'This time he's going to be,' Gunvald Larsson said.

She stared at him spitefully, her eyes moist. Larsson hurled questions at her.

'Luntmakargatan 57?'

'Yes. That's what I said, didn't I?'

'The house facing the street or the one across the yard?'

'Across the yard.'

'Which floor?'

'Second.'

'How big is the flat?'

'One room.'

'And kitchen?'

'No, no kitchen. Only one room.'

'How many windows?'

'Two.'

'Facing the yard?'

'No, sea view!'

Gunvald Larsson bit his lip in annoyance. The veins in his forehead swelled once more.

'Well now,' Melander said. 'He has a studio flat on the second floor with two windows facing the yard. Do you know for sure that he's there now?'

'Yes,' she said. 'I do.'

'Have you a key?' Melander asked kindly.

'No, there is only one.'

'And he's locked the door after him?' Martin Beck asked.

'Bet your sweet life he has.'

'Does the door open inwards or outwards?' Gunvald Larsson asked.

She thought hard.

'Inwards.'

'Quite sure?'

'Yes.'

'How many storeys in the house facing the yard?' Martin Beck asked.

'Oh, four or so.'

'And what's on the ground floor?'

'A workshop.'

'Can you see the entrance from the windows?' Larsson asked.

'No, the Baltic,' the girl retorted. 'A bit of the city hall too. And the royal palace.'

'That'll do,' Larsson snapped. 'Take her away.'

The girl made a violent gesture.

'One moment,' Melander said.

There was silence in the room. Gunvald Larsson looked expectantly at Melander.

'Can't I go?' the girl asked. 'You did promise.'

'Yes,' Melander answered. 'Of course you can go. We just have to check up first that you're right. For your own sake. Oh, one thing more.'

'Yes. What?'

'He's not alone in the room, eh?'

'No,' the girl said very quietly.

'What's your name, by the way?' Gunvald Larsson asked.

'None of your damn business.'

'Take her away,' Gunvald Larsson said.

Melander got up, opened the door to the next room and said:

'Rönn, we have a lady here, do you mind if she sits with you for a while?'

Rönn appeared in the doorway. His eyes and nose were red. He took in the scene.

'Not at all.'

'Blow your nose,' Larsson said.

'Shall I give her some coffee?'

'Good idea,' Melander said.

He held the door for her and said politely:

'This way, please.'

The girl got up and went out. In the doorway she stopped and gave Gunvald Larsson and Martin Beck a cold, hard stare. Evidently they had not succeeded in making her like them. Something wrong with our basic psychological training, Martin Beck thought.

Then she looked at Melander and said slowly:

'Who's going to get him?'

'We are,' Melander said kindly. 'That's what the police are for.'

She didn't move, but went on looking at Melander. At last she said:

'He's dangerous.'

'How dangerous?'

'Very dangerous. He shoots. He'll probably shoot me too.'

'Not for a long time,' Gunvald Larsson said.

She ignored him.

'He has two submachine guns in the room. Loaded. And an ordinary pistol. He has said . . .'

Martin Beck said nothing, but waited for Melander's reply, hoping that Gunvald Larsson would keep quiet.

'What has he said?' Melander asked.

'That he'll never let himself be taken alive. I know he means it.'

She still went on standing there.

'That's all,' she said.

'Thank you,' Melander said, closing the door after her.

'Huh,' Gunvald Larsson said.

'Fix the warrant,' Martin Beck said as soon as the door was shut. 'And out with the town plan.'

The blueprint of the town plan was on the desk before Melander had finished making the short phone call that gave them the legal right to do what they were about to do.

'It might be a bit tricky,' Martin Beck said.

'Yes,' Gunvald Larsson agreed.

He opened a drawer, took out his service pistol and weighed it for a moment in his hand. Martin Beck, like most Swedish plain-clothes policemen, carried a pistol in a shoulder holster in case he had to use it when on duty. Gunvald Larsson, on the other hand, had got himself a special clip with which he could fasten the holster to the waistband of his trousers. Slinging the pistol so that it hung by his right hip he said:

'Okay, I'll grab him myself. Coming?'

Martin Beck looked thoughtfully at Gunvald Larsson, who was a good half head taller than himself and looked gigantic now that he was standing up.

'It's the only way,' Larsson said. 'How else can we do it? Just imagine a horde of guys with submachine guns and tear-gas bombs and bullet-proof vests running in through that entrance and across the yard with him firing like a madman through the windows and out on to the staircase. Or are you yourself or the police commissioner or the prime minister or the king going to stand and shout through a megaphone, "You're surrounded. Better give yourself up."'

'Tear gas through the keyhole,' Melander said.

'That's an idea,' Gunvald Larsson said. 'But it doesn't appeal to me. Presumably the key's on the inside. No, plainclothes men in the street and two men go in. Coming?'

'Sure,' Martin Beck said.

He would rather have had Kollberg with him, but the mugger was without doubt Gunvald Larsson's man.

Luntmakargatan lies in the part of Stockholm known as Norrmalm. A long narrow street with mainly old buildings. It stretches from Brunnsgatan in the south to Odengatan in the north, with a lot of workshops on the street level and shabby dwellings in the houses across the yard.

They were there in less than ten minutes.

14

'Pity you don't have the computer with you,' Gunvald Larsson said. 'You could break the door down with it.'

'Yes,' Martin Beck said.

They parked the car in Rådmansgatan, went around the corner and saw several colleagues on the pavement near the entrance to number 57.

The arrival of the police did not seem to have attracted anyone's attention.

'We'll go in . . .' Gunvald Larsson began, and checked himself.

Perhaps he remembered his lower rank, for he looked at his wrist watch and said:

'I suggest I go in with you half a minute behind me.'

Martin Beck nodded, crossed the street, stood in front of the shop window of Gustaf Blomdin's jeweller's shop and watched an unusually beautiful old grandfather clock tick away thirty seconds. Then he turned on his heel, crossed the road diagonally without bothering about the traffic and entered the main doorway of number 57.

He crossed the yard without looking up at the windows, opened the door on to the staircase and went swiftly and quietly up the stairs. From the workshop on the ground floor came the muffled pounding of machinery.

The paint had flaked off the door of the flat; sure enough, it bore the name Simonsson. Not a sound could be heard from inside, nor from Gunvald Larsson, who was standing, quite still and straight, to the right of the door. He passed his fingers lightly across the cracked panelling.

Then he glanced inquiringly at Martin Beck.

Martin Beck regarded the door for a second or two and nodded. He stood to the left of it, tense and with his back to the wall.

Despite his height and weight, Gunvald Larsson moved very quickly and silently in his rubber-soled sandals. Supporting himself with his right shoulder against the wall opposite the door, he stood tensed for a few seconds. He had evidently made sure that the key was in the lock on the inside, and it was obvious that Rolf Lundgren's private world would not remain private much longer. Martin Beck barely had time to think this before Gunvald Larsson flung his fifteen stone against the door, crouching slightly and with his left shoulder forward.

The door flew open with a crash, wrenched off both lock and upper hinge, and Gunvald Larsson followed it into the room through a cascade of dry splinters. Martin Beck was only half a yard behind him, striding smoothly and swiftly. His pistol was raised.

The mugger was lying on his back in bed with his right arm locked under a woman's neck, but he managed to get it free, spin around and fling his upper body towards the floor and thrust his hand under the bed. When Gunvald Larsson struck him he was already kneeling with the submachine gun resting on the floor but with his right hand closed around the extended metal frame.

Gunvald Larsson struck him only once, with open hand and not very hard, but it was enough to make the mugger drop the weapon and tumble backwards against the wall, where he remained sitting with his left arm over his face.

'Don't hit me,' he said.

He was naked. The woman, who had leapt up from the bed a second later, was wearing a wrist watch with a tartan strap. She stood stock still with her back to the wall on the other side of the bed, staring from the submachine gun on the floor to the gigantic fair man in the tweed suit. She made not the slightest attempt to cover herself. She was a pretty girl with short hair and long, slim legs. She had young breasts with large, pale-brown nipples and a prominent dark line from the navel to the moist, dark-brown patch of hair around her private parts. She also had dark, bushy hair in her armpits. There was already goose-flesh on her thighs, arms and breasts.

A man from the workshop on the ground floor was gaping through the broken door.

Martin Beck was struck by the absurdity of the situation and for the first time in weeks he felt the corners of his mouth twitch. He was standing in the middle of a room in broad daylight pointing a 7.65-millimetre Walther at two naked people while a man in a blue carpenter's apron and with a foot-rule in his right hand stared at him in amazement.

He put his pistol away. A policeman appeared outside the door and told the workman to get a move on.

'What!' the girl exclaimed.

Gunvald Larsson looked at her with distaste and said:

'Get your clothes on.'

After a moment he added:

'If you have any.'

He was standing with his right foot on the submachine gun. With a glance at the mugger he said:

'You too. Get your clothes on.'

The mugger was a muscular, well-built young man with a fine suntan, apart from a narrow white band across his thighs, and with long fair hair on his arms and legs. He straightened up slowly, holding his right hand in front of his genitals, and said:

'That damn stinking little slut.'

Another policeman entered the room and stared. The girl still stood motionless with her palms pressed against the wall and her fingers wide apart, but the expression in her brown eyes showed that she was pulling herself together.

Martin Beck looked around the room and saw a blue cotton dress slung over the back of a kitchen chair. On the chair were also a pair of panties, a bra and a string bag. Under it, on the floor, was a pair of sandals. Handing her the dress he said:

'Who are you?'

The girl stretched out her right hand and took the dress but did not put it on. Looking at him with her clear brown eyes she said:

'My name's Lisbeth Hedvig Maria Karlström. Who are you?'

'A policeman.'

'I'm reading modern languages at Stockholm University and have passed my finals in English.'

'And this is what you learn at the university?' Gunvald Larsson said without turning his head.

'I came of age a year ago and I'm wearing a diaphragm.'

'How long have you known this man?' Martin Beck asked.

The girl still made no attempt to get dressed. Instead, she looked at her wrist watch and said:

'For exactly two hours and twenty-five minutes. I met him at the Vanadis Baths.'

In the other part of the room the man was fumbling putting on his underpants and khaki trousers.

'That's nothing much to show the ladies,' Gunvald Larsson said.

'You're a boor,' the girl said.

'Think so?'

Gunvald Larsson said this without taking his eyes off the mugger. He had looked at the girl only once.

'On with your shirt now,' he urged paternally. 'Now your socks. And shoes. That's a good boy.'

Two uniformed radio policemen had entered the room; they admired the scenery for a moment, then led the mugger away.

'Get dressed, please,' Martin Beck said to the girl.

At last she drew the dress over her head, went over to the chair, put on her panties and slipped her feet into the sandals. Rolled up the bra and put it in the string bag.

'What has he done?' she asked.

'Sex maniac,' Gunvald Larsson said.

Martin Beck saw her turn pale and swallow. She looked at him inquiringly. He shook his head. She swallowed again and said uncertainly:

'Shall I . . .'

'There's no need. Just give your name and address to the officer outside. Good-bye.'

The girl went out.

'You let her go!' Gunvald Larsson said in amazement.

'Yes,' Martin Beck said.

Then he shrugged and said:

'Let's go through things, shall we?'

15

Five hours later the time was half past five and Rolf Evert Lundgren had still admitted nothing but the fact that his name was Rolf Evert Lundgren.

They had stood around him, and sat opposite him, and he had smoked their cigarettes, and the tape recorder had turned and turned, and his name was still Rolf Evert Lundgren and anyway, it was on his driver's licence.

They had asked and asked and asked him questions, Martin Beck, and Melander, and Gunvald Larsson, and Kollberg, and Rönn, and even Hammar, who was now chief superintendent, had been in and looked at him and said one or two well-chosen words. His name was still Rolf Evert Lundgren and anyway it was on his driver's licence and the only thing that seemed to annoy him was when Rönn sneezed without holding a handkerchief to his mouth.

The absurd thing was that had it concerned only himself he could have pleaded not guilty for all they cared, right through every interrogation and every conceivable court of appeal and his entire prison sentence, for in the studio flat across the yard and in the built-in wardrobe they had found not only two submachine guns and a Smith and Wesson 38 Special but also objects which definitely bound him to four of the robberies, plus the bandanna handkerchief, the tennis shoes, the nylon pullover with the monogram on the breast pocket, two thousand preludin pills, the brass knuckles and several stolen cameras.

At six o'clock Rolf Evert Lundgren sat drinking coffee with Superintendent Martin Beck of the homicide squad and Detective Inspector Fredrik Melander. All three took two lumps of sugar and all three were equally glum and exhausted as they sipped at their paper mugs.

'The absurd thing is that if this had concerned only yourself we could have called it a day now and gone home,' Martin Beck said.

'I don't know what you're getting at,' Lundgren said.

'I mean what's so silly is . . .'

'Oh, stop nagging.'

Martin Beck made no reply; he sat quite still, staring at the arrested man. Melander said nothing either.

At six fifteen Martin Beck drank his coffee, which was now stone cold, crumpled up the mug and dropped it into the wastepaper basket.

They had tried persuasion, kindness, severity, logic, shock tactics; they had tried to get him to engage a lawyer and they had asked him ten times if he wanted anything to eat. In fact, they had tried everything except striking him. Martin Beck had noticed that Gunvald Larsson had been several times on the point of resorting even to this forbidden method but had realized that it wouldn't do to hit suspects, especially while superintendents and commissioners were running in and out of the room. At last this had annoyed Gunvald Larsson so much that he had gone home.

At half past six Melander also went home. Rönn came in and sat down. Rolf Evert Lundgren said:

'Put that filthy handkerchief away. I don't want your germs.'

Rönn, who was a mediocre policeman with mediocre imagination and a mediocre sense of humour, considered for a moment the possibility of being the first interrogator in the history of crime to extract a confession by sneezing, but refrained.

Of course the normal thing, Martin Beck thought, was to let the accused sleep on the matter. But was there time to sleep on the matter? The man in the green T-shirt and khaki trousers did not seem particularly sleepy and had not even mentioned the matter. Oh well, sooner or later they would have to let him rest.

'That lady who came here this morning,' Rönn said by way of introduction, and sneezed.

'That damn stinking little slut,' the accused muttered, sinking into a dejected silence.

After a while he said:

'She loves me, so she says. She says I need her.'

Martin Beck nodded. Another minute or so passed before the man went on:

'I don't love her. I need her about as much as I need dandruff.'

Don't nag, Martin Beck thought. Say nothing.

'I like to have decent girls,' Lundgren said. 'What I'd really like is *one* decent girl. Then to get picked up thanks to that jealous slut.'

Silence.

'Slob,' Lundgren muttered to himself.

Silence.

'She's good for only one thing.'

Sure, thought Martin Beck, but this time he was wrong. Thirty seconds later the man in the green T-shirt said:

'Okay.'

'Let's talk now,' Martin Beck said.

'Okay. But I want one thing straight first. That slut can give me an alibi for that business last Monday. In Tanto Park. I was with her then.'

'We know that already,' Rönn said.

'You do? Oh, so she did tell you that.'

'Yes,' Rönn said.

Martin Beck stared at him; so Rönn had not bothered to

mention this simple fact to anyone else in the department. He could not help saying:

'That's nice to know. It absolves Lundgren here from suspicion.'

'Yes, it does,' Rönn said calmly.

'Let's talk now,' Martin Beck said.

Lundgren eyed him narrowly.

'Not us,' he said.

'What do you mean?'

'Not *you*, I don't want to talk to you,' Lundgren explained.

'Who then?' Martin Beck asked patiently.

'With the guy that nabbed me. The tall one.'

'Where's Gunvald?' Martin Beck asked.

'Gone home,' Rönn replied with a sigh.

'Phone for him.'

Rönn sighed again. Martin Beck knew why. Gunvald Larsson lived at Bollmora, a suburb far to the south.

'He needs rest,' Rönn said. 'He's had a tiring day. Nabbing a big gangster like this.'

'Shut up,' Lundgren said.

Rönn sneezed and reached for the phone.

Martin Beck went into another room and called up Hammar, who said at once:

'Can this Lundgren be considered cleared of suspicion as regards the murder?'

'Rönn questioned his mistress earlier today. She seems able to give him an alibi for the murder in Tanto Park. As for Vanadis Park last Friday, of course, he hasn't one.'

'I grasp that,' Hammar said. 'What do you think yourself?'

Martin Beck hesitated before replying.

'I don't think he's the one.'

'You consider he's not the murderer?'

'I don't see how he can be. Nothing fits. Quite apart from the alibi for Monday, he's the wrong type. Sexually he seems quite normal.'

'I see.'

Even Hammar had seemed a trifle irritable. Martin Beck went back to the other two. Rönn and Lundgren were sitting in stony silence.

'Are you sure you don't want anything to eat?' Martin Beck asked.

'No,' Lundgren said. 'When's that guy coming?'

Rönn sighed and blew his nose.

16

Gunvald Larsson entered the room. Exactly thirty-seven minutes had passed since he had been called up and the taxi receipt was still in his hand. Since they had last seen him he had shaved and put on a clean shirt. He sat down at the desk opposite Rolf Lundgren, folded the receipt and put it in the top right-hand drawer. He was now ready for some of the two million four hundred thousand hours of overtime that the Swedish police have to put in annually. But in view of his rank it was uncertain if he would ever be paid for his work during the next few hours.

It was some little while before Gunvald Larsson said anything. He busied himself with the tape recorder, the note pad and his pencils. There was no doubt some sort of psychological reason for this, Martin Beck thought as he regarded his colleagues. He disliked Gunvald Larsson and had no high opinion of Rönn. He had no high opinion of himself either for that matter. Kollberg made out he was scared and Hammar had seemed irritated. They were all very tired, added to which Rönn had a cold. Many of the men in uniform on patrol duty, either on foot or in radio cars, were also working overtime and were also worn out. Some of them were scared and Rönn was certainly not the only one with a cold.

And in Stockholm and its suburbs by this time there were over a million frightened people.

The hunt was entering its seventh abortive day.

And they were the bulwarks of society.

Some bulwarks.

Rönn blew his nose.

'Well,' Gunvald Larsson said, laying one of his huge hairy hands on the tape recorder.

'It was you who picked me up,' Rolf Evert Lundgren said in a tone that was almost reluctant admiration.

'Yes,' Gunvald Larsson said, 'that's correct. But it's nothing I feel particularly proud of. It's my job. I pick up scum like you every day. By next week I'll probably have forgotten you.'

This of course was a qualified truth, but the bombastic opening evidently had some effect. The man called Rolf Evert Lundgren seemed to droop.

Gunvald Larsson switched on the tape recorder.

'What's your name?'

'Rolf Evert Lundgren.'

'Born?'

'Yes.'

'No insolence.'

'Fifth of January 1944.'

'Where?'

'In Gothenburg.'

'Which parish?'

'Lundby.'

'What are your parents' names?'

Come on now, Gunvald, Martin Beck thought. You've several weeks for that. There's only one thing that really interests us.

'Any previous convictions?' Gunvald Larsson asked.

'No.'

'Have you been at an approved school?'

'No.'

'We're chiefly interested in one or two details,' Martin Beck put in.

'Didn't I damned well say I'd only talk to him there?' Rolf Evert Lundgren said.

Gunvald Larsson looked stonily at Martin Beck and said:

'What's your occupation?'

'Occupation?'

'Yes, you have one, I presume?'

'Well . . .'

'What do you call yourself?'

'Businessman.'

'And what kind of business do you consider you do?'

Martin Beck and Rönn exchanged a resigned look. This was going to take time.

It took time.

One hour and forty-five minutes later Gunvald Larsson said:

'We're chiefly interested in one or two details.'

'So I gather.'

'You've already admitted having been in Vanadis Park on the evening of the ninth of June, that is, Friday of last week?'

'Yes.'

'And that you committed robbery with violence there at nine fifteen p.m.?'

'Yes.'

'Against Hildur Magnusson, shopkeeper?'

'Yes.'

'What time did you get to the park?' Rönn asked.

'Shut up,' Lundgren said.

'No insolence,' Gunvald Larsson said. 'What time did you get to the park?'

'About seven. A little after maybe. I left home when the rain eased off.'

'And you were in Vanadis Park from seven o'clock up to the time when you assaulted and robbed this lady, Hildur Magnusson?'

'Well, I was in the neighbourhood. Keeping an eye open.'

'Did you notice anyone else in the park during that time?'

'Yes, a few people.'

'How many?'

'Ten maybe. Or twelve. Ten more likely.'

'I presume that you observed these individuals closely?'

'Yes, pretty closely.'

'To see if you dared attack them?'

'Rather to see if they were worth the trouble.'

'Can you recollect any of these people you saw?'

'Well, one or two anyway.'

'Which ones?'

'I saw two cops.'

'Policemen?'

'Yes.'

'In uniform?'

'No.'

'Then how did you know they were policemen?'

'Because I'd already seen them twenty or thirty times. They work at the cop-shop at Surbrunnsgatan and drive a red Volvo Amazon and sometimes a green Saab.'

Now don't say 'The police station, you mean?' thought Martin Beck.

'The police station in ninth district, you mean?' said Larsson.

'Yes, if that's the one in Surbrunnsgatan.'

'What was the time when you saw these policemen?'

'About eight thirty, I should think. I mean, that's when they came.'

'How long did they stay?'

'Ten minutes, maybe fifteen. Then they drove to Lill-Jans Wood.'

'How do you know?'

'They said so.'

'Said so? Do you mean you spoke to them?'

'Like hell I did. I was standing nearby and heard what they said.'

Gunvald Larsson made a pregnant pause. It was not hard to imagine what he was thinking. At last he said:

'Who else did you see?'

'A guy and a girl. Pretty young. About twenty.'

'What were they doing?'

'Petting.'

'What?'

'Petting. He shoved his fingers up her cunt.'

'Mind your language.'

'What's wrong with it? I'm telling you just how it was.'

Gunvald Larsson was again silent for a moment. Then he said stiffly:

'Are you aware that a murder was committed in the park while you were there?'

Lundgren put his hand to his face. For the first time in many hours he seemed nervous and at a loss for an answer.

'I read about it,' he said at last.

'And?'

'It wasn't me. I swear. I'm not that sort.'

'You have read about this girl. She was nine years old and her name was Eva Carlsson. She was dressed in a blue skirt, striped T-shirt . . .'

Gunvald Larsson consulted his notes.

'. . . and black wooden-soled sandals. Did you see her?'

Lundgren did not answer. After about half a minute Larsson repeated the question.

'Did you see this girl?'

After a long hesitation Lundgren said:

'Ye-es, I think so.'

'Where did you see her?'

'In the playground down by Sveavägen. At any rate there was a kid there. A girl.'

'What was she doing?'

'Swinging.'

'Who was she with?'

'No one. She was solo.'

'What time was this?'

'Just after . . . soon after I got there.'

'And that was?'

'I'd say about ten past seven. Or a bit later.'

'And you're sure she was alone?'

'Yes.'

'And she had a blue skirt and striped T-shirt, you're sure of that?'

'No. I mean, I don't know. But . . .'

'But what?'

'I think so.'

'And you saw no one else? No one talking to her?'

'Wait,' Lundgren said. 'Wait, wait. I read about that in the paper. I've thought no end about it.'

'What have you thought?'

'Well, that I . . .'

'Did you speak to her yourself?'

'No, no, for Christ's sake.'

'She sat there all alone on the swings. Did you go up to her?'

'No, no . . .'

'Let him tell us himself, Gunvald,' Martin Beck said. 'He must have thought a lot about this.'

Lundgren glanced resignedly at Martin Beck. He looked tired and rather scared. No truculence now.

Keep quiet, Gunvald, Martin Beck thought.

Gunvald Larsson kept quiet.

The mugger sat silent for a minute or two, his head in his hands. Then he said:

'I've thought about this. Every day since then.'

Silence.

'I've tried to think back. I know that I saw that kid in the playground and that she was alone and that it must have been just after I got there. About ten or a quarter past seven. I didn't pay much attention, see. Only a kid, and anyway I wasn't going to work down there by the playground. Too near the street, Sveavägen. So I didn't think much about her. Then. It would have been different if she'd been in the playground up there by the water tower.'

'Did you see her there too?' Gunvald Larsson asked.

'No, no ...'

'Did you follow her?'

'No, no, try and get this. I wasn't in the least interested in her, but ...'

'But what?'

'There weren't many people in the park that evening. It was stinking weather, could have poured at any minute. I was about to give up and go home when that old bag ... when that lady came. But ...'

'But what?'

'What I want to say is that I saw that girl. And the time must have been nearly seven fifteen.'

'You've already said that. Who did you see with her?'

'No one. She was solo. What I mean is that I saw about a dozen people the whole time. I'm ... I'm very careful. When I work I don't want to get caught. So I watch out. And what I mean is that maybe one of those I saw ...'

'Well, whom did you see?'

'I saw those two cops ...'

'The policemen.'

'Yes, for Chrissake. One was red-haired and had a trenchcoat and the other had a cap and jacket and trousers, lean face sort of.'

'Axelsson and Lind,' Rönn said to himself.

'You're very observant,' Martin Beck said.

'Yes, you are,' Gunvald Larsson said. 'Out with the rest now.'

'Those two cops . . . no, don't interrupt, for Chrissake . . . they went into the park from different directions and were in there about a quarter of an hour. But it was much later than when I saw the girl. Must have been an hour and a half later.'

'And?'

'And then those other two. The guy that felt the girl up. That was earlier again. I followed them, was nearly going to have a go . . .'

'Have a go?'

'Yes, at . . . no, for Chrissake, I don't mean sex. The girl had on a mini-skirt, black and white, and the guy was wearing a blazer. Looked upper class, but she had no handbag.'

He was silent. Gunvald Larsson, Martin Beck and Rönn waited.

'She had white lace panties.'

'How could you see that without her seeing you?'

'She didn't see a damn thing, neither did the guy. They wouldn't have seen a hippopotamus. They didn't even see each other. And they must have come about . . .'

He paused. Then said:

'What time were the cops there?'

'Eight thirty,' Martin Beck said quickly.

The mugger looked almost triumphant as he said:

'Exactly. And by then those two had been gone at least a quarter of an hour. And the two of them were in the park for at least half an hour. From a quarter to eight until a quarter past, that is. I followed them at first, but then I shoved off. Stand there watching their petting. Christ no. But when they came the little girl wasn't there. She wasn't in the playground, either when they came or when they left. I'd have seen her if she'd been there. I'd have noticed.'

He was really trying to help now.

'So she was in the playground at seven fifteen but had gone by seven forty-five?' Gunvald Larsson said.

'Exactly.'

'And what did you do in the meantime?'

'Kept an eye open, so to speak. I hung about the corner, between Sveavägen and Frejgatan. So that I could see people entering the park from those directions.'

'Just a moment. You say you saw about ten people altogether?'

'In the park? Yes, roughly.'

'Two policemen, this young couple, the lady you robbed, the little girl. That's six.'

'I also followed a man with a dog. I followed him the whole time, but he only walked about by Stefan's Church and near the street. Probably waiting for the dog to shit or something.'

'What direction did this man come from?' Martin Beck asked.

'He came in from Sveavägen, by the sweet kiosk.'

'What time?' Rönn asked.

'It was soon after I came. He was the only one I considered before that guy with the girl. He . . . wait, he came in by the sweet kiosk and had one of those skinny little dogs. The girl was in the playground then.'

'Are you sure?' Gunvald Larsson said.

'Yes. Wait a sec now. I followed him the whole time. He was there for ten minutes or a quarter of an hour. And when he left, the girl must have gone.'

'What other people did you see?'

'Only a few tramps.'

'Tramps?'

'Yes. I never even considered them. Two or three of them. They went through the park.'

'Try and remember now, for God's sake,' Gunvald Larsson said.

'I am trying. I saw two walking together. They came from Sveavägen and went up towards the water tower. Dossers. Pretty old.'

'Are you sure they were together?'

'Almost. I'd seen them before. I remember now thinking they had a bottle of booze or a few beers they wanted a swig at up in the park. But that happened while those two were still there, the girl with the lace panties and her guy, the ones who were petting. And . . .'

'Yes?'

'I saw another one. He came from the other direction.'

'A tramp too, as you call it?'

'Well, it wasn't anyone worth noticing anyway, not as far as I was concerned. He came from up by the water tower. I remember quite plainly now, I remember thinking he must have come up the steps from Ingemarsgatan. Hell of a steep pull, climbing up that way and then just going down again.'

'Down again?'

'Yes. He went out into Sveavägen.'

'When did you see him?'

'Soon after the man with the dog had gone.'

There was silence in the room. It dawned on them one by one what Lundgren had just said.

It dawned on Lundgren himself last of all. Raising his eyes, he looked Gunvald Larsson straight in the face.

'Christ, yes!'

Martin Beck felt a nerve tingle somewhere in his system. And Gunvald Larsson said:

'To sum up, we can say this: An elderly, well-dressed man with a dog entered Vanadis Park from Sveavägen some time between seven fifteen and seven thirty. He walked past the sweet kiosk and the playground, where the girl still was. The man with the dog stayed for about ten minutes, fifteen at the most, in that part of the park that lies between Stefan's Church and Frejgatan. You shadowed him the whole time. When he came back and went out of the park, again past the sweet kiosk and the playground, the girl was no longer in the playground. A few minutes later a man appeared from the direction of the water tower and went out into Sveavägen. You presumed that he had come from Ingemarsgatan and climbed the steps behind the water tower and then come down through the park in the direction of Sveavägen. But this man could just as well have come from the direction of Sveavägen a quarter of an hour earlier, while you were shadowing the man with the dog.'

'Yes,' Lundgren said, gaping.

'He could have passed the playground and lured the girl with him up to the water tower. He could have killed her there and thus been on the way back when you saw him.'

'Yes,' Lundgren said, gaping wider.

'Did you see which way he went?' Martin Beck asked.

'No, all I thought was he'd left the park and that was that.'

'Did you see him at close quarters?'

'Yes, he went right past me. I was standing behind the sweet kiosk.'

'Good, let's have his description,' Gunvald Larsson said. 'What did he look like?'

'He wasn't very tall, not small either. Rather shabby. He had a big nose.'

'How was he dressed?'

'Shabbily. Light-coloured shirt, white I should think. No tie. Dark trousers, grey or brown, I think.'

'And his hair?'

'A bit thin. Brushed straight back.'

'Hadn't he a coat?' Rönn put in.

'No. Neither jacket nor overcoat.'

'Colour of eyes?'

'What?'

'Did you see the colour of his eyes?'

'No. Blue, I imagine. Or grey. He was that type. Fair.'

'How old could he have been?'

'Oh, between forty and fifty. Nearer forty, I should think.'

'And his shoes,' Rönn said.

'Don't know. Though probably those ordinary black shoes that tramps usually have. But that's only a guess.'

Summing up, Gunvald Larsson said:

'A man aged about forty, normal build, average height, with thin hair brushed back and big nose. Blue or grey eyes. White or light-coloured shirt, unbuttoned. Brown or dark-grey trousers, probably black shoes.'

Martin Beck was vaguely reminded of something, but the thought vanished as soon as it came. Larsson went on:

'Presumably black shoes, oval face ... Good. Only one thing more. You're to look at some pictures. Bring the vice squad's album.'

Rolf Evert Lundgren looked through the pages of photographs of known sexual perverts. He examined each picture carefully and shook his head each time.

He could find nobody resembling the man he had seen in Vanadis Park.

Moreover, he was quite sure that the man he had seen was not among the photographs in the register.

It was already midnight when Gunvald Larsson said:

'Now we'll see that you get something to eat and then you can sleep. See you tomorrow. That's all for today.'

He seemed almost jaunty.

The last thing the mugger said before being led away was:

'Just think, I saw the bastard!'

He too seemed almost jaunty.

Yet he himself had been very near to killing several people, and as recently as twelve hours earlier he had been ready to shoot down both Martin Beck and Gunvald Larsson, if only he had had the chance.

Martin Beck pondered this.

He also reflected that they had a description – and a poor one at that – which fitted many thousands of people. Still, it was something.

And the hunt entered its seventh day.

There was something else at the back of Martin Beck's mind, but he didn't know what it was.

He had coffee with Rönn and Gunvald Larsson before they went home.

They exchanged some concluding remarks.

'Do you think it took a long time?' Gunvald Larsson asked.

'Yes,' Martin Beck said.

'Yes, I did,' Rönn agreed.

'Well, you see,' Gunvald Larsson said pompously, 'you have to go carefully and start at the beginning. Establish a confidential relationship.'

'Yes,' Rönn said.

'Frankly, I thought it took a hell of a long time all the same,' Martin Beck said.

Then he drove home. Had another cup of coffee and went to bed.

Lay awake in the dark, thinking.

Of something.

17

Martin Beck felt anything but rested when he awoke on Friday morning. In fact he felt more tired than he had done when, after far too many cups of coffee, he had at last got to sleep late the night before. He had slept fitfully, tossing and turning, and had had one nightmare after the other. He woke up with a dull ache in his midriff.

At breakfast he had a violent quarrel with his wife about something so trivial that he had already forgotten the cause of it when he closed the front door behind him five minutes later. Anyway, his part in the quarrel had been somewhat passive; his wife had been the one to take the offensive.

Tired, dissatisfied with himself, his eyelids smarting, he took the subway to Slussen, changed trains and went on to Midsommarkransen to pay a short visit to his office in Västberga Allé. He disliked using the underground, and although it was quicker to go by car from Bagarmossen to the southern police headquarters, he refused obstinately to become a motorist. This was one of the seeds of dissension between him and Inga, his wife. Moreover, since finding out that the state pays a policeman who uses his own car forty-six öre a kilometre, she had raised the question more and more often.

He took the lift to the third floor, pressed the buttons of the numerical code on the keypad outside the glass doors, nodded to the doorman and went into his office. From the pile on his desk he sorted out the papers he was to take along to the headquarters in Kungsholmsgatan.

On the desk was also a postcard in vivid colours with a picture of a donkey in a straw hat, a chubby little dark-eyed girl with a basket of oranges and a palm tree. It had been posted in Mallorca, where the youngest man in the department, Ake Stenström, was on holiday, and it was addressed to 'Martin Beck and the boys'. It took Martin Beck some time to decipher what he had written with a smeary ball-point pen:

> Are you wondering what has become of all the pretty chicks? They have found out my whereabouts! How are you managing without me? Badly, I presume. But hold out, maybe I'll come back! Ake

Martin Beck smiled and put the postcard in his pocket. Then he sat down, looked up the number of the Oskarsson family and reached for the phone.

The husband answered. He said that the rest of the family had just come home and that if Martin Beck wanted to see them he had better come as soon as possible, as they had a lot to do before going away.

He ordered a taxi and ten minutes later he rang the doorbell of the Oskarssons' flat. The husband opened the door and showed him to the sofa in the bright living room. The children were not there, but he heard their voices from one of the other rooms. Their mother stood by the window ironing, and when Martin Beck came in she said:

'Excuse me, but I've nearly finished.'

'I'm so sorry I have to disturb you,' Martin Beck said. 'But I'd very much like to talk to you once more before you go away.'

The husband nodded and sat down in a leather armchair on the other side of the low coffee table.

'Naturally we want to do all we can to help,' he said. 'My wife and I know nothing, but we've talked to Lena and it seems as if she doesn't know any more than what she has already told you. Unfortunately.'

His wife put down the iron and looked at him.

'Thank heavens, I'd rather say.'

She pulled out the plug of the iron and sat down on the arm of her husband's chair. He put his arm around her hips.

'I really came to ask whether your son has by any chance said anything that might have a bearing on what happened to Annika?'

'Bosse?'

'Yes, according to Lena he disappeared for a while and there's nothing to indicate that he didn't follow Annika. He may even have seen the person who brought about her death.'

He heard how idiotic he sounded and thought: I'm talking like a book. Or like a police report. How the hell do I think I'm going to get anything sensible out of a three-year-old?

The couple in the armchair did not seem to react to his stilted speech. They probably took it for granted that police always spoke like that.

'But a policewoman has already been here and talked to him,' Mrs Oskarsson said. 'He's so young.'

'Yes, I know,' Martin Beck said. 'But I thought I'd ask to try all the same. He might just have seen something. If we could get him to remember that day . . .'

'But he's only three,' she broke in. 'He can't even talk properly. We're the only ones who can understand all he says. Come to that, we don't understand everything either.'

'Well, we can try,' the husband said. 'I mean, let's do what we can to help. Perhaps Lena can get him to remember what he did.'

'Thanks,' Martin Beck said. 'I'd be grateful.'

Mrs Oskarsson got up and went into the nursery, returning soon with the children.

Bosse ran up and stood beside his father.

'What's that?' he asked, pointing to Martin Beck.

He put his head on one side and looked at him. His mouth was dirty and he had a scratch on his cheek and a large bruise was visible under the fair hair that hung down over his forehead.

'Daddy, what's that?' he repeated impatiently.

'It's a man,' his father explained, giving Martin Beck an apologetic smile.

'Hello,' Martin Beck said.

Bosse ignored the greeting.

'What her name?' he asked his father.

'His,' Lena corrected.

'My name's Martin,' Martin Beck said. 'What's yours?'

'Bosse. What name?'

'Martin.'

'Mattin. Name Mattin,' Bosse said in a tone indicating amazement that anyone could have a name like that.

'Yes,' Martin Beck said. 'And your name's Bosse.'

'Daddy's name Kurt, Mommy's name . . . what name?'

He pointed to his mother, who said:

'Ingrid, you know that.'

'Ingy.'

He went up to the sofa and laid a chubby and sticky hand on Martin Beck's knee.

'Have you been in the park today?' Martin Beck asked.

Bosse shook his head and said shrilly:

'Not play park. Go for drive!'

'Yes,' his mother said soothingly. 'Later. Later we'll go for a drive.'

'Then you too drive,' Bosse said challengingly to Martin Beck.

'Yes. Perhaps.'

'Bosse can drive,' the boy said with satisfaction, climbing on to the sofa.

'What do you do when you play in the park?' Martin Beck asked in a tone which he himself thought sounded ingratiating and affected.

'Bosse not play park. Bosse drive,' the boy said in fury.

'Yes, of course,' Martin Beck said. 'Of course you're going for a drive.'

'Bosse's not going to play in the park today,' his sister said. 'The man only asked what you did last time you played in the park.'

'Silly man,' Bosse said with emphasis.

He slid down off the sofa and Martin Beck regretted not having brought some sweets for the boy. He didn't usually bribe witnesses in order to win them over, but on the other hand he had never before had a three-year-old witness to question. A slab of chocolate now would surely have done the trick.

'He says that about everyone,' Bosse's sister said. 'He's so silly.'

Bosse hit out at her and said indignantly:

'Bosse not silly! Bosse good!'

Martin Beck felt in his pockets to see if he had anything that might interest the lad, but found only the picture postcard from Stenström.

'Look at this,' he said.

Bosse ran up to him at once and looked eagerly at the postcard.

'What's that?'

'A postcard,' Martin Beck replied. 'Can you see what's on it?'

'Horse. Flower. Andrin.'

'What's andrin?' Martin Beck asked.

'Mandarin,' his mother explained.

'Andrin,' Bosse said, pointing. 'And flower. And horse. And girl. What name girl?'

'I don't know,' Martin Beck said. 'What do you think her name is?'

'Ulla,' Bosse replied promptly. 'Girl Ulla.'

Mrs Oskarsson nudged her daughter.

'Do you remember when Ulla and Annika and Bosse and Lena were in the park on the swings?' Lena asked quickly.

'Yes!' Bosse said delightedly. 'Ulla, Annika, Bosse, Lena swing in park buy ice cream. Member?'

'Yes,' Lena said. 'Do you remember we met a dog in the park?'

'Yes! Bosse meet little dog. Not pat little dog. Dang'ous pat little dog. Member?'

The parents exchanged a glance and the mother nodded. Martin Beck realized that the boy really did recall that very day in the park. He sat quite still, hoping that nothing would make the boy lose the thread.

'Do you remember,' his sister went on, 'Ulla, Lena, Bosse play hopscotch?'

'Yes,' Bosse said. 'Ulla, Lena hopscotch. Bosse too hopscotch. Bosse know hopscotch. Member Bosse hopscotch?'

The boy's delighted answers to his sister's questions came promptly, and the dialogue followed a pattern which made Martin Beck suspect that this was a question game that brother and sister used to play, a kind of do-you-remember game.

'Yes,' Lena said, 'I remember. Bosse, Ulla, Lena played hopscotch. Annika didn't play hopscotch.'

'Annika not want hopscotch. Annika cross Lena, Ulla,' Bosse said gravely.

'Do you remember that Annika got cross? Annika got cross and went off.'

'Lena, Ulla silly Annika.'

'Did Annika say that Lena and Ulla were silly? Do you remember that?'

'Annika said Lena, Ulla silly.'

And then very emphatically:

'Bosse not silly.'

'What did Bosse and Annika do when Lena and Ulla were silly?'

'Bosse, Annika hide-and-scck.'

Martin Beck held his breath, hoping that the girl knew what she should ask next.

'Do you remember when Bosse and Annika played hide-and-seek?'

'Yes. Ulla, Lena not to play hide-and-seek. Ulla, Lena silly. Annika good. Bosse good. Man good.'

'Which man?'

'Man in park good. Bosse got ticker.'

'Did the man give you a ticker in the park? Do you remember?'

'Man give Bosse ticker.'

'Do you mean a watch like Daddy's, that goes tick-tick?'

'Ticker!'

'What did the man say? Did the man speak to Bosse and Annika?'

'Man speak Annika. Man give Bosse ticker.'

'Did Bosse and Annika get ticker from the man?'

'Bosse get ticker. Annika not ticker. Bosse get ticker.'

Bosse turned suddenly and ran over to Martin Beck.

'Bosse get ticker!'

Martin Beck drew back his cuff and showed Bosse his wrist watch.

'Do you mean a ticker like this? Is this what the man gave you?'

Bosse hit Martin Beck's knee.

'No! Ticker!'

Martin Beck turned to the boy's mother.

'What is ticker?' he asked.

'I don't know,' she said. 'He does say that for watches and clocks, but he doesn't seem to mean that now.'

Bending down to the little boy he asked:

'What did Bosse and Annika and the man do? Did you both play with the man?'

Bosse seemed to have lost interest in the question game and said sulkily:

'Bosse can't find Annika. Annika silly play man.'

Martin Beck opened his mouth to say something but shut it again when he saw the witness dart out of the room.

'Can't catch me! Can't catch me!' the boy shouted gaily.

His sister looked after him crossly and said:

'He's always so silly.'

'What do you think he meant by ticker?' the father asked.

'I don't know. Evidently not a watch, anyway. I don't know,' she said.

'It seems as if he met someone together with Annika,' Mr Oskarsson said.

But when? thought Martin Beck. On Friday or a fortnight ago?

'Ugh, how horrible,' his wife said. 'It must have been that man. The one who did it.'

She shuddered and her husband stroked her back soothingly. He gave Martin Beck a worried look and said:

'He's so small. He knows so few words. I hardly think he's able to give any kind of description of this man.'

Mrs Oskarsson shook her head.

'No,' she said. 'Not unless there was something special about his appearance. If he'd had some kind of uniform, for instance, Bosse would no doubt have called him the sojer. Otherwise I don't know. Children are never surprised at anything. If Bosse were to meet a man with green hair and pink eyes and three legs he wouldn't think anything of it.'

Martin Beck nodded.

'Perhaps he did have a uniform. Or something else that Bosse remembers. It might be better if you talked to him alone?'

Mrs Oskarsson got up and shrugged.

'I'll try by all means.'

She left the door ajar so that Martin Beck could hear her conversation with the boy. After twenty minutes she came back, having been unable to get anything more out of him.

'Can't we leave now?' she asked anxiously. 'I mean, does Bosse have to . . .'

She broke off, then went on:

'And Lena?'

'Yes, go by all means,' Martin Beck said, getting up.

He shook hands and thanked them both, but as he was going Bosse came running out and flung his arms around his legs.

'Not go. You sit there. You must talk Daddy. Bosse also talk you.'

Martin Beck tried to free himself but Bosse had a tight grip and Martin Beck did not want to upset him. Feeling in his trouser pocket he took out a fifty-öre bit and looked inquiringly at the mother. She nodded.

'Here, Bosse,' he said, showing the boy the coin.

Bosse let go at once, took the money and said:

'Bosse buy ice cream. Bosse has lots money buy ice cream.'

He ran ahead of Martin Beck out into the hall and took down a little jacket that was hanging on a hook low down near the front door. The boy dug into the jacket pockets.

'Bosse has lots money,' he said, holding up a grubby five-öre bit.

Martin Beck opened the door, turned around and held out his hand to Bosse.

The little boy stood hugging the jacket, and when he pulled his hand out of the pocket a little bit of white paper fluttered down to the floor. Martin Beck stooped to pick it up and the boy shouted:

'Bosse's ticker! Bosse get ticker man!'

Martin Beck looked at the piece of paper in his hand.

It was an ordinary underground ticket.

18

A good deal had already happened on this Friday morning, 16 June 1967.

The police sent out a description which had the disadvantage of fitting tens of thousands of more or less blameless citizens.

Rolf Evert Lundgren had slept on the matter and wanted to bargain. If the police would let bygones be bygones he offered to take part in the search and to give 'supplementary information', whatever that might be. Having received a flat refusal, he sank into gloomy meditation and at last asked of his own accord to talk to a lawyer.

One of the detectives persisted in pointing out that Lundgren still lacked an alibi for the evening of the murder in Vanadis Park and in questioning his reliability as a witness. This in its turn led to Gunvald Larsson making a woman extremely embarrassed and to another woman making Kollberg, if possible, even more embarrassed.

Gunvald Larsson dialled a telephone number to a flat near Vanadis Park. The following conversation ensued:

'Jansson speaking.'

'Good morning. This is the police, homicide squad, Detective Inspector Larsson.'

'Oh yes.'

'May I speak to your daughter, please? Majken Jansson.'

'Certainly. Just a moment. We're having breakfast. Majken!'

'Hello. This is Majken Jansson speaking.'

The voice was bright and cultured.

'This is the police. Detective Inspector Larsson.'

'Oh yes.'

'You have stated that you took a breath of air in Vanadis Park on the evening of the ninth of June.'

'Yes.'

'What were you wearing when you took this breath of air?'

'What was I . . . Well, let me see, I had on a black-and-white cocktail dress.'

'What else?'

'A pair of sandals.'

'Aha. What else?'

'Nothing. Quiet, Daddy, he's only asking what I . . .'

'Nothing? You had nothing else on?'

'N-no.'

'I mean, didn't you by any chance have anything under your dress?'

'Yes. Yes of course. Naturally I had underclothes.'

'Aha. And what kind of underclothes?'

'What kind of underclothes?'

'Yes, exactly.'

'Well, naturally I had what . . . well, what one usually has. Oh, Daddy, it's the *police*.'

'And what do you usually have?'

'Well, a bra naturally and . . . well, what do you think?'

'I don't think anything. I have no preconceived opinions. I am merely asking.'

'Panties of course.'

'I see. And what kind of panties?'

'What kind? I don't know what you mean. I had panties of course, knickers.'

'Panties?'

'Yes. I'm sorry but . . .'

'And what did these panties look like? Were they red or black or blue or maybe patterned?'

'A pair of . . .'

'Yes?'

'A pair of white lace panties. Yes, Daddy, I'll ask him. Why on earth are you asking me all this?'

'I am just checking the evidence of a witness.'

'The evidence of a *witness?*'

'Exactly. Good-bye.'

Kollberg drove to an address in the Old Town, parked the car at Storkyrkobrinken and climbed a worn, winding stone staircase. He looked for a doorbell which wasn't there and then, true to habit, he pounded deafeningly on the door.

'Come in!' a woman's voice called.

Kollberg went in.

'Good Lord,' she said. 'Who are you?'

'Police,' he said lugubriously.

'Well, let me say that the police have a helluva nice habit of . . .'

'Is your name Lisbeth Hedvig Maria Karlström?' Kollberg asked, looking demonstratively at the piece of paper in his hand.

'Yes. Is it about that business yesterday?'

Kollberg nodded and looked about him. The room was untidy but pleasant. Lisbeth Hedvig Maria Karlström was wearing a blue-striped pyjama jacket, which came down only far enough to show that she had not even lace panties on underneath. She had evidently just got up. She was making coffee, stirring it with a fork to make it drip more quickly through the filter bag.

'I've just got up and am making coffee,' she said.

'Oh.'

'I thought it was the girl who lives next door. She's the only one who ever thumps on the door like that. And at this hour. Like some?'

'What?'

'Coffee.'

'Well . . .' Kollberg said.

'Do sit down.'

'What on?'

She pointed with the fork to a leather-covered ottoman beside the exceedingly unmade bed. He sat down dubiously. She put the coffeepot and two cups on a tray, pushed forward a small, low table with her left knee, put the tray down and sat on the bed, crossing her legs and thus revealing quite a lot of her anatomy, which was not altogether without its charms.

She poured out the coffee and handed a cup to Kollberg.

'Thank you,' he said, looking at her feet.

He was a suspectible person and at the moment felt strangely disturbed. In some way she reminded him far too much of someone, probably his wife.

She gave him a worried look and said:

'Would you like me to put something more on?'

'It might be just as well,' Kollberg said thickly.

She got up at once, went over to the closet, took out a pair of brown corduroy slacks and pulled them on. Then she unbuttoned the pyjama jacket and took it off. For a moment she stood with her upper body naked – with her back to him, to be sure, but that hardly improved matters. After a short hesitation she pulled a knitted sweater over her head.

'It's just that it makes me so damned hot,' she said.

He drank some coffee.

'What do you want to know?' she asked.

He drank some more.

'Very nice,' he said.

'It's just that I don't know anything. Nothing at all. It was a lousy business, with that Simonsson, I mean.'

'His name was Rolf Evert Lundgren,' Kollberg said.

'Oh, that too. You must think I seem . . . that I don't appear in a very good light. But there's nothing I can do about it. Now.'

She looked about her unhappily.

'Perhaps you'd like to smoke?' she asked. 'I'm afraid I haven't any cigarettes. I don't smoke myself.'

'Nor do I,' Kollberg said.

'Oh. Well, bad light or not, it can't be helped. I met him at the Vanadis Baths at nine o'clock and then I went home with him. I know nothing at all.'

'Presumably you do know one thing that interests us.'

'What would that be?'

'How was he? Sexually, I mean?'

She shrugged awkwardly. Took a piece of crispbread and began nibbling it. At last she said:

'No comment. I don't as a rule . . .'

'What don't you as a rule?'

'I don't as a rule comment on men I go with. If you and I, for instance, got into bed together now, I wouldn't go around afterwards giving people details about you.'

Kollberg fidgetted. He felt hot and upset. He wanted to take off his coat. It was even possible that he wanted to take off his clothes altogether and have sex with this girl. True, he had very seldom done so while on duty and particularly not since he had got married, but it had happened.

'I'd be very glad if you would answer this question,' he said. 'Was he normal, sexually?'

She did not answer.

'It's important,' he added.

She looked him straight in the eyes and said gravely:

'Why?'

Kollberg looked at the girl doubtfully. It was a hard decision and he knew that many of his colleagues would consider his next

115

words more blameworthy than if he had undressed and got into bed with her.

'Lundgren is a professional criminal,' he said at last. 'He has confessed to about a dozen violent assaults. Last Friday evening – a week ago, that is – he is known to have been in Vanadis Park at the same time as a little girl was murdered there.'

She looked at him quickly and swallowed several times.

'Oh,' she said softly. 'I didn't know that. I would never have thought that.'

After a moment she looked at him again with her clear brown eyes and said:

'That answers my question. Now I see that I must answer yours.'

'Well?'

'As far as I could judge he was completely normal. Almost too normal.'

'What do you mean by that?'

'I mean that I too am completely normal sexually but that ... well, since I do it fairly seldom I want a little more than ... shall we say routine?'

'I see,' Kollberg said, scratching behind his ear with embarrassment.

He hesitated a few seconds. The girl regarded him gravely. At last he said:

'Was it he who ... approached you in the Vanadis Baths?'

'No, the reverse, if anything.'

She got up abruptly and went over to the window, which looked out on to the cathedral. Without turning her head she said:

'Exactly. The reverse, if anything. I went out yesterday to pick up a man. I was prepared for it, had prepared myself, if you like.'

She shrugged.

'That's the way I live,' she said. 'I've done so for several years and if you like I'll tell you why I live like that.'

'It's not necessary,' Kollberg said.

'I don't mind,' she said, fingering the curtain. 'Telling you, I mean . . .'

'It's not necessary,' Kollberg repeated.

'At any rate I can assure you that he behaved quite normally together with me. At first he didn't even seem . . . particularly interested. But . . . I saw to it that he became so.'

Kollberg drank up his coffee.

'Well, that's about all,' he said uncertainly.

Still without turning around, she said:

'I've had things happen before, but this really makes me think. It's not at all nice.'

Kollberg said nothing.

'Nasty,' she said to herself, again fingering the curtain.

Then she turned around and said:

'I assure you it was I who took the initiative. In a very flagrant manner. If you like I'll . . .'

'No, you needn't.'

'And I can assure you that he was absolutely normal when he . . . when we were in bed together.'

Kollberg got up.

'I think you're very nice,' she said spontaneously.

'I like you too,' he said.

He walked over to the door and opened it. Then to his own astonishment he said:

'I'm married. Have been for over a year. My wife's expecting a baby.'

She nodded.

'As regards the life I lead . . .'

She broke off.

'It's not so good,' he said. 'It can be dangerous.'

'I know.'

'So long,' Kollberg said.

'So long,' said Lisbeth Hedvig Maria Karlström.

He found a parking ticket on his car. Absentmindedly he folded up the yellow slip and put it in his pocket. Nice girl, he thought. Looks rather like Gun, I wonder why . . .

As he settled down behind the wheel he reflected that the whole thing was verging on the perfect parody of a really bad novel.

At headquarters Gunvald Larsson said heartily:

'That settles it. He's sexually normal and his reliability as a witness is confirmed. Waste of time, the whole thing.'

Kollberg was not altogether sure that it *had* been a waste of time.

'Where's Martin?' he asked.

'Out interrogating infants,' Gunvald Larsson said.

'And otherwise?'

'Nothing.'

'Here's something,' Melander said, looking up from his papers.

'What?'

'A summary from the psychologists. Their viewpoints.'

'Humph,' Gunvald Larsson snorted. 'Unrequited love for a wheelbarrow and all that rot.'

'Well, I'm not so sure,' Melander mumbled.

'Take the pipe out of your mouth so that we can hear what you say,' Kollberg said.

'They have an explanation here, an explanation that seems very plausible. It's rather worrying.'

'Can things be more worrying than they are already?'

'As regards the possibility that this man is not in our records,' Melander went on impassively. 'They say that he might very well have a clean police record. That he might even have lived for a long time without giving any expression at all to his inclinations. That the satisfaction of sexual perversion in many ways resembles addiction to drugs. This is borne out by foreign examples. Someone who is a sexual pervert can behave for year after year as an exhibitionist or a Peeping Tom and in that way find an outlet for his sex urge. But if that individual, on a sudden impulse, commits a rape or a sex murder, the only way he can get satisfaction in future is to commit more rapes and more murders.'

'Like the old story about the bear,' Gunvald Larsson said. 'A bear that has once killed a cow, and so on.'

'It's the same with a junkie who wants stronger and stronger drugs the whole time,' Melander said, riffling through the report. 'A junkie who starts off with hashish and then changes to heroin can't go back to hashish because he gets no kick out of it any more. It may be the same sort of thing with a sexual pervert.'

'It sounds sensible,' Kollberg said. 'But elementary.'

'I think it sounds damned unpleasant,' Gunvald Larsson said.

'It's much more unpleasant than that,' Melander said. 'It says here that a person can have lived for many years without giving any noticeable expression to his perverted sex urge, he needn't even have masturbated or looked at dirty pictures, still less have behaved as an exhibitionist or a Peeping Tom. He can simply have sat thinking of different forms of perversion, without actually knowing about it himself, until suddenly a chance impulse triggers off an act of violence. Then he just can't help repeating it, over and over again, with growing ruthlessness and presumably increasing bestiality.'

'Rather like Jack the Ripper,' Gunvald Larsson said.

'What about the impulse?' Kollberg asked.

'It can be triggered by all kinds of things – a chance situation, a state of mental weakness, illness, alcohol, drugs. If this view of crime is admissible, then there are no clues to the criminal in his own past. The police registers are useless, the same as the case histories of hospitals and doctors. The individual in question just isn't there. And once he has started raping or killing, he can't stop. He's also incapable of giving himself up or of controlling his own actions.'

Melander sat in silence for a moment. Then he tapped with his knuckles on the xeroxed report and said:

'There's something in this that fits our case horribly well.'

'I imagine there are dozens of other explanations,' Gunvald Larsson said irritably. 'It might be a stranger, for instance, a foreigner just passing through. It might even be two different murderers; what happened in Tanto Park was perhaps a murder done on the spur of the moment – an impulse caused by the publicity around the first one.'

'There's a lot against that line of reasoning,' Melander said. 'Knowledge of the locality, the somnambulant certainty with which the murder was carried out, the choice of time and place, the absurd fact that after two murders and seven days of searching we haven't found a single suspect worth mentioning. Unless we count that man Eriksson. And there's a detail that rather discounts the theory of an impulse murder: in both cases the girl's panties were missing. That information has not been given out to the press.'

'I imagine there are other explanations all the same,' Gunvald Larsson said surlily.

'I'm afraid that's wishful thinking,' Melander said, lighting his pipe.

'Yes,' Kollberg said, rousing himself. 'It may be wishful thinking, Gunvald, but I do hope you're right. Otherwise . . .'

'Otherwise,' Melander said, 'we have nothing at all. The only thing that can lead us to the murderer is to catch him red-handed next time. Or . . .'

Kollberg and Larsson each completed the thought and arrived at the same unpleasant conclusion.

'Or for him to repeat the murder over and over again with the same sleepwalking certainty until his luck gives out and we catch him,' Melander said.

'What else does it say there?' Kollberg asked.

'The usual rigmarole. A whole lot of contradictory speculations. He can be oversexed or undersexed – the latter seems to be the most probable. But there are also examples of the reverse.'

Putting down the report Melander said:

'Has it occurred to you that even if we saw him standing here in front of us we have no proof that he committed these two murders. The only material we have is some very dubious footprints in Tanto Park. And the only thing actually proving that the person we're after is a man is a few spermatozoa on the ground near the girl's body, again in Tanto Park.'

'And if he's not in our records we wouldn't even be helped by a full set of fingerprints,' Kollberg said.

'Exactly,' Melander said.

'But we have a witness,' Gunvald Larsson said. 'The mugger saw him.'

'If only we could rely on that,' Melander said.

'Couldn't you say one little tiny thing to cheer us up?' Kollberg asked.

Melander made no answer and they lapsed into silence. In the room next door they heard the telephones ring and Rönn and someone else answer.

'What did you think of that girl?' Gunvald Larsson asked suddenly.

'I liked her,' Kollberg said.

At the same instant yet another unpleasant thought occurred to him. He knew whom Lisbeth Hedvig Maria Karlström had reminded him of. Not his wife, far from it. She reminded him in an ominous way of a person whom he had never met during her lifetime but who had governed his thoughts and actions long after she was dead. He had seen her only once, in the mortuary at Motala on a summer's day three years ago.

He shook himself, ill at ease.

A quarter of an hour later Martin Beck walked in with the ticket.

19

'What's that?' Kollberg asked.

'A ticket,' Martin Beck replied.

Kollberg looked at the crumpled ticket lying in front of him on the desk.

'An underground ticket,' he said. 'So what? If you want your travelling expenses reimbursed you must go to the cashier's office.'

'Bosse, our three-year-old witness, got it from a man that he and Annika met in Tanto Park just before she died,' Martin Beck said.

Melander shut the door of the filing cabinet and came up to them. Kollberg turned his head and stared at Martin Beck.

'Just before the man strangled her, you mean,' he said.

'Maybe. The question is: What can we get out of this ticket?'

'Fingerprints, perhaps,' Kollberg said.

Melander leaned forward, muttering, while he studied the ticket.

'Possible but hardly probable,' Martin Beck said. 'First of all the person who tore it off the block touched it, then whoever gave it to the boy must have touched it, I grant you, but the boy has had it in his pocket since Monday together with snails and God knows what, and to my shame I've touched it too. Apart from that, it's crumpled and fluffy. We'll try, of course. But look at the punch holes first.'

'I've already looked,' Kollberg said. 'It's punched at one thirty p.m. on the twelfth, it doesn't say which month. That can mean . . .'

He broke off and all three thought what it might mean. Melander was the one to speak.

'These one-krona tickets, type 100, are used only within the actual city limits,' he said. 'It may be possible to find out when and where it was sold. There are two other numbers on it.'

'Ring Stockholm Tramways,' Kollberg said.

'It's called Stockholm Local Transport now,' Melander said.

'I know. But the uniform buttons still have ST on them. I suppose they can't afford to make new ones. How the hell is that possible when it costs a krona to go from Gamla Stan to Slussen – the next station? What does a button cost?'

Melander was already on his way into the next room. The ticket still lay on the desk, presumably he had photographed it in his mind with serial number and everything. They heard him lift the receiver and dial a number.

'Did the boy say anything else?' Kollberg asked.

Martin Beck shook his head.

'Only that. That he was with the girl and that they met a man. He just found the ticket by chance.'

Kollberg tipped back his chair and bit his thumbnail.

'So we have a witness who has presumably both seen and spoken to the murderer. It's just that this witness is only three years old. Had he been a little older . . .'

'The murder would never have happened,' Martin Beck broke in. 'At any rate not then and there.'

Melander came back.

'They said they'd call up soon.'

The call came through a quarter of an hour later. Melander listened and made notes. Then he said thank you and hung up.

Sure enough, the ticket had been bought on 12 June. It had

123

been sold by a ticket office cashier at the northern barrier of the underground station at Rådmansgatan. In order to pass that barrier one has to go down through one of the two entrances on either side of Sveavägen on a level with the School of Economics.

Martin Beck knew the Stockholm underground network very well but he still went over and looked at the wall map.

If the person who bought the ticket at Rådmansgatan was on his way to Tanto Park, he must change trains either at T-Centralen, Gamla Stan or Slussen. In that case he would come to Zinkensdamm. From there it was about five minutes' walk to the spot where the dead girl had been found. The journey had been started between one thirty and one forty-five and should have taken about twenty minutes, allowing for changing trains. Between five minutes to two and ten minutes past the person in question could therefore have arrived at Tanto Park. According to the doctor the girl had probably died between two thirty and three o'clock, possibly a little earlier.

'As regards time it fits,' Martin Beck said.

At the same second Kollberg said:

'It fits as regards time. If he went straight there.'

Haltingly, as though speaking to himself, Melander said:

'The station isn't so far from Vanadis Park.'

'No,' Kollberg said. 'But what does that tell us? Nothing. That he rides on the underground from park to park and kills little girls? Come to that, why didn't he take the 55 bus? He could have gone all the way and not had to walk.'

'And probably been caught,' Melander said.

'Yes,' Kollberg agreed. 'There are never many people on that bus. They recognize the passengers.'

Sometimes Martin Beck wished that Kollberg were not quite so talkative. He wished it now, as he licked and stuck down the envelope with the ticket. He had tried to hold on to a thought that flashed past; had Kollberg kept quiet he might have succeeded. Now the moment had gone.

Having sent off the envelope he called up the laboratory and asked to have the result as soon as possible. The man who answered was called Hjelm and Martin Beck had known him for many years. He sounded rushed and was in a bad mood. He asked if the gentlemen at Kungsholmsgatan and Västberga Allé knew how much he had to do. Martin Beck said he quite realized that their burden of work was inhuman and that he would gladly come along and give a hand if only he were skilled enough to carry out such exacting work. Hjelm muttered something and promised to deal with the ticket right away.

Kollberg went out to lunch and Melander shut himself up with his piles of papers. Before doing so he said:

'We have the name of the cashier who sold the ticket at Rådmansgatan. Shall I get someone to talk to her?'

'By all means,' Martin Beck said.

He sat down at the desk, glanced through his papers and tried to think. He felt irritable and nervy and presumed that fatigue was to blame. Rönn stuck his head in, looked at him and vanished without a word. Otherwise he was left in peace. Even the telephone was silent for a long time. Just as he was on the verge of dozing off at his desk, something which had never happened before, the phone rang. Before picking up the receiver he looked at the time. Twenty minutes past two. Still Friday. Bravo, Hjelm, he thought.

It was not Hjelm but Ingrid Oskarsson.

'Sorry to disturb you,' she said. 'You must be awfully busy.'

Martin Beck mumbled some kind of answer and heard himself how unenthusiastic he sounded.

'But you said I was to ring. It may not be important, but I thought I'd better tell you.'

'Yes, of course, forgive me, I didn't hear who it was,' Martin Beck said. 'What has happened?'

'Lena suddenly remembered something Bosse said in the park on Monday. When that happened.'

'Oh? What?'

'She says he told her he had met his day daddy.'

'Day daddy?' he asked.

And thought: Are there such things?

'Yes. Bosse was with a day mother during the daytime earlier this year. There are so few day nurseries and I didn't know what to do with him while I was at work. So I advertised and found a day mother for him in Timmermansgatan.'

'But didn't you just say "day daddy"?'

'No, no, what I meant was, this day mother had a husband, he wasn't there all day but he often came home early, so Bosse saw him nearly every day. And he started calling him day daddy.'

'And Bosse told Lena that he met him in Tanto Park on Monday?'

Martin Beck felt his tiredness vanish. Reaching for the note pad he felt in his pocket for a pen.

'That's right,' Mrs Oskarsson said.

'Did Lena gather whether it was before or after the time he was missing?'

'She's sure he didn't say it until afterwards. That's why I thought I'd better tell you. I don't suppose it has anything to do with it at all, he seemed so nice and kind, that man. But if Bosse met him, perhaps he in his turn might have seen or heard something ...'

Martin Beck put pen to paper and asked:

'What's his name?'

'Eskil Engström. He's a lorry driver, I think. They live in Timmermansgatan. I've forgotten the number, can you wait a second and I'll have a look.'

She came back a minute later and gave him an address and telephone number.

'He seemed such a nice man,' she said. 'I saw him quite often when I called for Bosse.'

'Did Bosse say anything more about this meeting with the day daddy?'

'No. And we've tried to get him to tell us about it now, but he seems to have forgotten it.'

'What does the man look like?'

'Well, it's hard to say. Pleasant. Bit down at heel, perhaps, but that may be due to his job. He's about forty-five or fifty, thin-haired. Looks very ordinary.'

There was silence for a while as Martin Beck made notes. Then he said:

'If I understand rightly, you don't leave Bosse with this day mother any more?'

'No. They've no children of their own, it was so dull for him. I was promised a vacancy at a day nursery, but a mother who was a nurse got it instead. They have priority around here.'

'Where is Bosse now in the daytime?'

'At home. I had to give up my job.'

'When did you stop leaving him with the Engströms?'

She thought for a moment and then said:

'The first week in April. I had a week off then. When I started work again Mrs Engström had taken a new day child and couldn't have Bosse.'

'Did Bosse like being with her?'

'Fairly well. I think he liked Mr Engström best. The day daddy, that is. Do you think he was the one who gave Bosse the ticket?'

'I don't know,' Martin Beck replied. 'But I'll try and find out.'

'I want to help all I can,' she said. 'We're going away this evening, you know that?'

'Yes, I know. Hope you have a nice trip. Say hello to Bosse for me.'

Martin Beck put down the receiver, thought for a moment, lifted it again and rang the vice squad.

While waiting for the information he had asked for, he pulled over one of the files lying on the desk and turned the pages until he came to the transcript of the nocturnal interrogation with Rolf

Evert Lundgren. He carefully read Lundgren's scant description of the man he had seen in Vanadis Park. Mrs Oskarsson's description of the day daddy was still less detailed, but there was a faint possibility that it might be the same person.

There was no Eskil Engström in the vice squad's records.

Martin Beck closed the file and went into the adjoining room. Gunvald Larsson sat behind his desk, staring broodingly out of the window and picking his teeth with the paper knife.

'Where's Lennart?' Martin Beck asked.

Gunvald Larsson reluctantly finished his dental research, wiped the paper knife on his sleeve and said:

'How the hell do I know?'

'Melander then?'

Gunvald Larsson put the paper knife down on the pen tray and shrugged.

'In the lavatory, I suppose. What do you want?'

'Nothing. What are you doing?'

Gunvald Larsson did not answer at once. Not until Martin Beck moved towards the door did he say:

'People are bloody mental.'

'What do you mean?'

'I've just been talking to Hjelm. He wants a word with you, by the way. Well, one of the men at Maria police station finds a pair of women's panties in the shrubbery at Hornstulls Strand. Without telling us he goes and hands them in to the forensic laboratory, saying that they may be the panties that were missing from the body in Tanto Park. So the boys at the lab stand there staring at a pair of outsize pink pants too big even for Kollberg and wondering what the hell it's all about. Can you blame them. How stupid can you get in this job?'

'I've often asked myself the same thing,' Martin Beck said. 'What else did he say?'

'Who?'

'Hjelm.'

'For you to call him up when you'd finished your little chat on the phone.'

Martin Beck went back to his temporary desk and called the forensic laboratory.

'Oh yes, your underground ticket,' Hjelm said. 'We couldn't develop any worthwhile fingerprints, the paper's too fluffy.'

'I was afraid of that,' Martin Beck said.

'We're not quite finished with it yet. I'll send the usual report later. Oh yes, we did find some blue cotton fibre, presumably from the lining of a pocket.'

Martin Beck thought of the little blue jacket that Bosse had clasped in his arms. He thanked Hjelm and put down the receiver. Then he called a taxi and put on his coat.

It was Friday, and the big weekend exodus out of the city had already begun, although it was still fairly early in the afternoon. The traffic moved sluggishly over the bridges and despite the driver's skilful and shrewd manoeuvring, the taxi took nearly half an hour to reach Timmermansgatan, on the south side.

The house was near the southern railway station. It was old and dilapidated and the entrance was dark and chilly. There were only two doors on the ground floor; one of them opened on to a paved courtyard with dustbins and a frame on which carpets were beaten. Martin Beck could just make out the name ENGSTRÖM on the tarnished brass plate on the second door. The bell button was missing and he knocked loudly on the panel of the door.

The woman who opened the door was about fifty. She was small and lean and was wearing a brown woollen dress and slippers made of floral turkish towelling. She peered doubtfully at Martin Beck through noticeably thick spectacles.

'Mrs Engström?'

'Yes,' she replied in a voice that seemed far too rough to be coming from such a frail woman.

'Is Mr Engström at home?'

'N-no,' she said slowly. 'What do you want?'

'I'd like a word with you. I know one of your day children.'

'Which one?' she asked suspiciously.

'Bo Oskarsson. His mother gave me your address. May I come in?'

The woman held open the door and he went through the little hall, past the kitchen and into the flat's one room. Outside the window he saw the dustbins and the carpet frame. A sofa-bed cluttered with ill-assorted cushions dominated the sparsely furnished room. Martin Beck saw nothing to indicate that children were ever there.

'I'm sorry,' the woman said, 'but what have you come about? Has anything happened to Bosse?'

'I'm a policeman,' Martin Beck said. 'It's purely a routine matter. Nothing to worry about. And Bosse's quite all right.'

The woman seemed rather frightened at first, then she seemed to brighten up.

'Why should I worry?' she said. 'I'm not afraid of the police. Is it to do with Eskil?'

Martin Beck smiled at her.

'Yes, Mrs Engström, I really came to speak to your husband. It seems, by the way, that he met Bosse the other day.'

'Eskil?'

She looked at Martin Beck in distress.

'Yes,' he said. 'Do you know when he will be home?'

She stared at Martin Beck with round blue eyes, which looked unnaturally large through the thick lenses.

'But . . . but Eskil's dead,' she said.

Martin Beck stared back. It was some moments before he recovered himself and was able to say:

'Oh, I'm sorry, I didn't know. I'm awfully sorry. When did it happen?'

'On the thirteenth of April this year. A car crash. The doctor said he didn't have time to think much before the end.'

The woman went up to the window and stared out at the dismal yard. Martin Beck looked at her bony back in the dress that was a size too large.

'My deepest sympathy, Mrs Engström,' he said.

'Eskil was on his way to Södertälje with his lorry,' she went on. 'It was a Monday.'

She turned around and said in a firmer voice:

'Eskil drove a lorry for thirty-two years with a clean licence. It wasn't his fault.'

'I see,' Martin Beck said. 'I'm awfully sorry to have troubled you. There must be some mistake.'

'And the hooligans who crashed into him were let off lightly,' she said. 'Even though the car was stolen.'

She nodded with a faraway look in her eyes. Went up to the settee and fiddled with the cushions.

'I'll go now,' Martin Beck said.

He was suddenly overcome by claustrophobia. He would have liked to have walked straight out of the gloomy room with the dreary little woman, but he controlled himself and said:

'If you don't mind, I'd be glad if I could see a photograph of your husband before I go.'

'I have no photo of Eskil.'

'But you've a passport, haven't you? Or a driver's licence?'

'We never travelled anywhere so Eskil didn't have a passport. And the driver's licence is very old.'

'May I see it?' Martin Beck asked.

She opened a drawer and took out the licence. It was made out in the name of Eskil Johan Albert Engström and had been issued in 1935. The photo showed a young man with shiny, wavy hair, big nose and a small mouth with thin lips.

'He didn't look like that later,' the woman said.

'How did he look? Can you describe him?'

She didn't seem at all surprised at the question but answered promptly:

'He wasn't as tall as you but a good bit taller than me. And rather thin. His hair was turning grey and had started to fall out. I don't know what else to say. He had a nice appearance – at least I thought so. Though you couldn't call him handsome, with his big nose and small mouth. But he looked *nice*.'

'Thank you, Mrs Engström,' Martin Beck said. 'I've disturbed you long enough.'

She saw him to the door and did not shut it until the street door had closed behind him.

Martin Beck took a deep breath and strode quickly along the street, northward, longing to get back to his desk.

On it lay two brief messages.

The first one was from Melander: *The woman who sold the underground ticket is called Gunda Persson. Remembers nothing. No time to look at the passengers, she says.*

The other was from Hammar: *Come at once. Urgent.*

20

Gunvald Larsson stood at the window studying six road workmen, who in their turn were studying a seventh, who was leaning on a shovel.

'Reminds me of a story,' he said. 'We lay in Kalmar once with a minesweeper. I was sitting in the navigation cabin together with the second mate and the boy on watch came in and said, "Please, sir, there's a dead man on the quayside." "Nonsense," I said. "Yes, sir," he said, "there's a dead man on the quayside." "Dead men don't stand about on quaysides," I said, "you must pull yourself together, Johansson." "But sir," he said, "it must be a dead man, I've been watching him all the time and he hasn't moved for several hours." And the second mate got up and looked out of the port-hole and said, "Hah, it's a council workman."'

The man in the street let the shovel fall and went off with the others. It was five o'clock and still Friday.

'Nice job if you can get it,' Gunvald Larsson said. 'Just stand there staring.'

'What are you doing yourself?' Melander asked.

'Standing and staring of course. And if the assistant commissioner had his office across the street I bet you anything he would stand in the window staring at me, and if the commissioner was on the floor above here he would stand staring at the assistant commissioner and if the home secretary . . .'

'Answer the phone instead,' Melander said.

Martin Beck had just entered the room. He stood by the door looking thoughtfully at Gunvald Larsson, who was just saying:

'What do you want me to do about it? Send out the dog van?'

He banged down the receiver, stared at Martin Beck and said: 'What's up with you?'

'You said something just now that made me think of . . .'

'The dog van?'

'No, something you said just before that.'

'What did it make you think of?'

'I don't know. It's something I can't call to mind.'

'You're not alone in that,' Gunvald Larsson said.

Martin Beck shrugged.

'There's to be a roundup tonight,' he said. 'I was just talking to Hammar.'

'Roundup? But everyone's already worn out,' Gunvald Larsson said. 'What will they look like tomorrow?'

'Doesn't seem very constructive,' Melander said. 'Whose idea is it?'

'I don't know. Hammar didn't seem very happy about it either.'

'Who's happy nowadays,' Gunvald Larsson said.

Martin Beck had not been there when the decision was made and had he had a chance he would probably have opposed it. He suspected that the motive was aimlessness in the investigative work and a general feeling that something must be done. The position was indeed very serious; the newspapers and television worked the public up with their vague accounts of the search, and people began saying that 'the police did nothing' or 'were helpless'. Seventy-five men were now working in the actual search force and the external pressure they were subjected to was enormous. Tips were pouring in every hour and every single one had to be checked, even though it could be seen at a glance that most of them were useless. Added to this was the internal pressure, the knowledge that the murderer not only must be caught but that he must be caught quickly. The investigation was a macabre race with death, and so far there was very little to go on. A vague description based on the evidence of a three-year-old child and a ruthless criminal. A underground ticket. A general idea of the mentality of the man they were hunting. The whole lot intangible and very disturbing.

'This isn't an investigation, it's a guessing game,' Hammar had said in regard to the underground ticket.

While this was one of his pet phrases and Martin Beck had heard it often before, it was an apt description of the situation at the moment.

Of course there was just a chance that a big roundup might give a clue, but the possibility seemed remote. The latest roundup had been made as late as Tuesday night and it had failed in its main purpose: to catch the mugger. Against that it had resulted in the seizure of about thirty criminals of various kinds, mainly drug dealers and burglars. This had further increased the burden of work for the police and moreover had caused panic in the underworld.

The roundup tonight meant that many would be jaded tomorrow. And tomorrow perhaps . . .

But a roundup it was to be and a roundup it was. It started about eleven o'clock and the news spread like wildfire through squats and drug dens. The result was discouraging. Thieves, fences, pimps, prostitutes, all lay low, even most of the junkies. Hour after hour passed and the raid continued with undiminished strength. They caught a burglar red-handed and a fence who had not enough instinct of self-preservation to go to earth. All that the police really succeeded in doing was to stir up the dregs – the homeless, the alcoholics, the drug addicts, those who had lost all hope, those who could not even crawl away when the welfare state turned the stone over. A fourteen-year-old schoolgirl was found naked in an attic. She had taken fifty preludin pills and been raped at least twenty times. But when the police came she was alone. Bleeding, filthy and bruised. She could still talk and gave a rambling account of what had happened, saying she didn't care. They couldn't even find her clothes but had to wrap her in an old quilt. They drove her to an address she gave and a person who made out she was her mother said that she had been missing for three days and refused to let her in. Only when the girl collapsed on the stairs did they send for an ambulance. Several similar cases came to light.

At half past four Martin Beck and Kollberg were sitting in a car at Skeppsbron.

'There's something funny about Gunvald,' Martin Beck said.

'Yes, he's stupid,' Kollberg said.

'No, something else. Something I can't put my finger on.'

'Oh?' said Kollberg with a yawn.

Just then an alarm came through on the radio.

'This is Hansson of fifth district. We're in Västmannagatan. We've found a body here. And . . .'

'Yes?'

'He fits the description.'

They drove straight there. A couple of police cars were drawn up in front of a condemned house. The dead man lay on his back in a room on the third floor. It was extraordinary that he had been able to get up there, for the house was half pulled down and most of the stairs were missing. Martin Beck and Kollberg climbed a light-metal ladder that the police had put up. The man was about thirty-five, with a striking profile, light-blue shirt and dark-brown trousers. Worn-out black shoes. No socks. Thin hair brushed back. They looked at him, someone stifled a yawn.

'Nothing to do but rope off and wait for the technical division to open up,' Kollberg said.

'Hardly worth waiting for,' said Hansson, who was an old hand. 'Suffocated by vomit. Clear as daylight.'

'Yes, it looks like it,' Martin Beck said. 'How long do you think he's been dead?'

'Not very long,' Kollberg said.

'No,' Hansson said. 'Not in this heat.'

An hour later Martin Beck went home and Kollberg went to Kungsholmsgatan.

They exchanged a few remarks before parting.

'The description did fit.'

'It fits a damn sight too many,' Martin Beck answered.

'And it's the right district.'

'We must find out who he is first.'

The time was half past six when Martin Beck got home to Bagarmossen. His wife had evidently just woken up. At any rate she was awake and still lay in bed. She looked critically at him and said:

'What a sight you look.'

'Why aren't you wearing a nightie?'

'It's so hot. Does it offend you?'

'No, I don't mind.'

He felt unshaven and frowzy but was too tired to do anything about it. Got undressed and put on his pyjamas. Got into bed. Thought: damn stupid idea this double bed, next pay day I'll buy a divan and put it in the other room.

'Does it get you all excited perhaps?' she said sarcastically.

But he was already asleep.

At eleven o'clock the same morning he was back at Kungsholmsgatan, somewhat hollow-eyed, but bathed and slightly refreshed. Kollberg was still there, and the dead man in Västmannagatan had not yet been identified.

'Not a paper of any kind in his pockets, not so much as an underground ticket.'

'What does the doctor say?'

'Suffocated by vomit, not a doubt. Thinks it's antifreeze. There was an empty can there.'

'How long had he been dead?'

'Twenty-four hours at the outside.'

They sat silent for a moment.

'I don't think he's the one,' Kollberg said.

'Nor do I.'

'But you never know.'

'No.'

Two hours later the mugger was confronted with the body.

'Christ, how disgusting,' he said.

And a moment later:

'No, it wasn't him I saw. I've never seen this guy before.'

Then he began to feel sick.

A real tough guy, thought Rönn, who was handcuffed to him and therefore had to accompany him to the lavatory. But he said nothing, merely took a towel and wiped Lundgren's mouth and forehead.

At investigation headquarters Kollberg said:

'There's no certainty, all the same.'

'No,' Martin Beck agreed.

21

The time was a quarter to eight on Saturday evening when Kollberg's wife called up.

'Hello, Kollberg,' he said, picking up the phone.

'What in heaven's name are you up to, Lennart? You haven't been home since yesterday morning.'

'I know.'

'I don't want to nag, but I hate being out here all by myself.'

'I know.'

'I want you to know that I'm not cross and I don't want to seem fretful, but I'm so lonely. I'm a tiny bit scared too.'

'I see. Okay, I'll come home now.'

'You're not to come just for my sake, not if there's something else you must do. As long as I can talk to you for a while.'

'Yes, I'll come now. At once.'

There was a short pause. Then she said with unexpected gentleness:

'Lennart?'

'Yes?'

'I saw you on TV not long ago. You looked so tired.'

'I am tired. I'll come home now. So long.'

'So long, darling.'

Kollberg said a few words to Martin Beck, then he went straight down to his car.

Like Martin Beck and Gunvald Larsson, he lived to the south of the city, but rather more centrally. At Palandergatan near the Skärmarbrink underground station. He drove straight through the city but when he got to Slussen he turned off to the right along Hornsgatan instead of continuing south. It was not difficult for him to analyse his own action.

There was no private life any longer, no time off, no room for thought of anything but duty and responsibility. So long as the murderer was at large, so long as it was light, so long as there was a park, and so long as a child might be playing there, then only the investigation mattered.

Or rather, the hunt. For a police investigation implies that one has factual material to work with, and the few facts available had long since been ground to pieces in the investigation machinery.

He thought of the conclusions in the psychological analysis; the murderer was a figure with no features and no qualities, and the only aim was to seize him before he had time to commit another murder. In order to do this they must be lucky, one of the reporters had said after the evening's press conference. Kollberg knew that this was an erroneous line of reasoning. He also knew that when the murderer was caught – and he was quite certain that he would be – it would look like luck and would be regarded by many people as a fluke. But it was a case of giving luck a helping hand, of making the net of circumstance that was eventually to catch the criminal as fine-meshed as possible. And this was a task that rested on him. And on every other policeman. Not on any outsider.

That is why Kollberg did not drive straight home, although he had fully intended doing so. Instead, he drove slowly west along Hornsgatan.

Kollberg was very methodical and considered that the taking of chances had no part in police work. He thought, for instance, that Gunvald Larsson had been guilty of a grave mistake when he broke into the mugger's flat, even if the door had been old and rickety. Supposing the door had not given at the first assault? Breaking open a door was taking a chance, and was therefore something of which he disapproved on principle. It even happened that he differed from Martin Beck on this point.

He drove around Mariatorget, closely observing the small groups of youngsters in the gardens and around the kiosks. He knew that this was mostly where schoolchildren and other young people met the small-scale drug dealers. Every day large quantities of hashish, marijuana, preludin and LSD were passed furtively from seller to buyer. And the buyers were getting younger and younger. Soon they would become addicts. Only the day before he had heard that schoolgirls of ten and eleven were offered shots. And there was nothing much the police could do; they just hadn't the resources. And to make quite sure that vice was bolstered up and those who indulged in it were still further lulled into boastfulness and smug security, this fact was trumpeted out time and again by the country's mass communication media. Anyway, he doubted whether this was a concern of the police at all. Drug-taking among young people was caused by a catastrophic philosophy which had been provoked by the prevailing system. Consequently society should be duty bound to produce an effective counterargument. One that was not based on smugness and more police officers.

Likewise he couldn't see the point of striking demonstrators at Hötorget and outside the US Trade Centre with sabres and truncheons, though he quite well understood those colleagues who were more or less forced to do so.

Detective Inspector Lennart Kollberg was thinking all this as he turned off down Rosenlundsgatan and Sköldgatan and drove past the miniature golf course at Tantogården. He parked the car and walked along one of the paths leading up into the park.

The daylight was fading and there were not many people about.

141

But naturally a few children were still playing, in spite of everything; come to that you could hardly expect all the children in a big city to be kept indoors just because a murderer was at large. Kollberg went and stood in one of the few sparse shrubberies, putting his right foot up on the stub of a tree. From this vantage point he could see the allotment gardens and the spot where the dead girl had lain five days earlier.

He was not aware of any special reason why he had been drawn to this particular place; perhaps because it was the biggest park in the central part of the city and was within easy reach on his way home. In the distance he saw several children, fairly big, perhaps in their early teens. He stood still, waiting. For what, he didn't know, perhaps for the children to go home. He was very tired. Now and then he saw a flickering in front of his eyes.

Kollberg was unarmed. Even with the growing gangster mentality and the steadily increasing brutality of crime, he was one of those who urged that the police should be disarmed entirely, and nowadays he carried a pistol only in case of extreme need and then only when directly ordered to do so.

A train trundled past on the high track, and only when the thud of the wheels on the joints began to die away did Kollberg realize that he was no longer alone in the shrubbery.

Then he was lying headlong in the dew-wet grass with the taste of blood in his mouth. Someone had struck him over the back of the neck, very hard and presumably with some kind of weapon.

Whoever struck Kollberg made a mistake. Similar mistakes had been made before, and several people had paid dearly for them.

Moreover, the assailant had put the weight of his body behind the blow and was off balance, and it took Kollberg less than two seconds to roll over on his back and bring his attacker to the ground – a tall, heavy man who fell with a thud. That was all Kollberg had time to take in, for there was a second man, who,

142

his face blank with astonishment, stuck his right hand into his jacket pocket and looked just as amazed when Kollberg, with one knee still on the ground, seized his arm and twisted it.

It was a grip that would have dislocated the arm or even broken it, if Kollberg had not checked himself halfway and contented himself with flinging the man backwards into the bushes.

The man who had struck him was sitting on the ground making faces while he rubbed his right shoulder with his left hand. The rubber truncheon had dropped from his hand. He was dressed in a blue track suit and looked several years younger than Kollberg. The second man crawled out of the bushes. He was older and smaller, and was wearing a corduroy jacket and sports trousers. Both had white sneakers with rubber soles. They looked like a couple of amateur yachtsmen.

'What the hell's all this?' Kollberg asked.

'Who are you?' asked the man in the track suit.

'Police,' Kollberg replied.

'Oh,' the smaller man said.

He had got up and was sheepishly dusting down his trousers.

'Then I presume we must apologize,' the first man said. 'A good trick that, where did you learn it?'

Kollberg made no reply. He had caught sight of a flat object on the ground. He stooped down and picked it up, and saw at once what it was. A small black automatic pistol, an Astra, made in Spain. Kollberg weighed it in his hand and looked suspiciously at the two men.

'Just what the hell is all this?' he said.

The big man stood up and shook himself.

'As I said, we apologize. You stood here behind the bushes spying on the children. And . . . you know, the murderer . . .'

'Yes? Go on.'

'We live up here,' the smaller man said, pointing to the block of flats on the other side of the railway line.

'And?'

143

'We have children of our own and we know the parents of the girl who was murdered the other day.'

'And?'

'And so as to help . . .'

'Yes?'

'We have formed our own voluntary civic guard that patrols in the park.'

'You have what?'

'We have formed a voluntary militia . . .'

Kollberg was overcome by a sudden rage.

'What the hell are you saying, man?' he roared.

'Don't stand there shouting at us,' the older man said angrily. 'We're not a couple of drunks that you can bully and push around in the cells. We're decent people with a sense of responsibility. We must protect ourselves and our children.'

Kollberg stared at him. Then he opened his mouth to bellow but controlled himself with an effort and said as quietly as he could:

'Is this your pistol?'

'Yes.'

'Have you a licence?'

'No. I bought it in Barcelona some years ago. I keep it locked in a drawer normally.'

'Normally?'

The black-and-white patrol van from Maria police station drove into the park with headlights full on. It was nearly dark now. Two policemen in uniform got out.

'What's going on here?' one of them said.

Then, recognizing Kollberg, he repeated in a different tone:

'What's going on here?'

'Take these two with you,' Kollberg said tonelessly.

'I've never set foot in a police station in my life,' said the older man.

'Nor have I,' said the one in the track suit.

'Then it's about time you did,' Kollberg said.

He paused for a moment, looked at the two policemen and said:

'I'll be along soon.'

Then he turned on his heel and walked off.

At Maria police station in Rosenlundsgatan there was already a line of drunks.

'What am I to do with these two civil engineers?' asked the police inspector on duty.

'Search them and put them in the cells,' Kollberg said. 'I'm taking them along to headquarters later.'

'You'll be sorry for this,' said the man in the track suit. 'Do you know who I am?'

'No,' Kollberg said.

He went into the guardroom to phone and as he dialled the number to his home he gazed mournfully at the ancient interior. He had done patrol duty here once; it seemed a very long time ago, but even then this district had been one of the worst for drunkards. Nowadays there was a better class of people living round about, but the district still came a good third in drunkard statistics after Klara and Katarina.

'Kollberg,' his wife said, answering the phone.

'I'll be a bit late,' he said.

'You sound so funny, is anything wrong?'

'Yes,' he said. 'Everything.'

He put the phone down and sat without moving for a moment. Then he called up Martin Beck.

'I was struck down from behind in Tanto Park a while ago,' he said. 'By two armed civil engineers. They've formed a militia here.'

'Not only there,' Martin Beck said. 'An hour ago a pensioner was battered in Haga Park. He was standing having a leak. I just heard about it.'

'Everything's going to hell.'

'Yes,' Martin Beck said. 'Where are you now?'

145

'Still at Maria. Sitting in an interrogation room.'

'What have you done with those two?'

They're in the cells here.'

'Bring them along.'

'Okay.'

Kollberg went down into the cell block. Many of the cells were already occupied. The man in the track suit stood staring out through the steel bars. In the next cell sat a tall, lean man aged about thirty-five with his knees drawn up to his chin. He was singing mournfully and sonorously:

'My wallet is empty, my heart is full of pain . . .'

The singer glanced at Kollberg and said:

'Hi, marshal, where's your six-shooter?'

'Haven't got one,' Kollberg said.

'This is the goddam wild west,' said the guard.

'What have you done?' Kollberg asked.

'Nothing,' the man said.

'It's true,' the guard said. 'We're letting him out soon. Some naval police brought him here. Five of them, can you imagine. He had annoyed some bo'sun or other on guard at Skeppsholmen. And they go and lug him all the way here. Idiots. Said they couldn't find a police station any closer. I had to shut him up in order to get rid of them. As if there wasn't enough already . . .'

Kollberg went on to the next cell.

'Now you've set foot in a police station,' he said to the man in the track suit. 'In a little while you'll see what it's like at head-quarters as well.'

'I shall report you for breach of authority.'

'I don't think you will,' Kollberg said.

He took out his notebook.

'But before we go I want the names and addresses of everyone in your organization.'

'We don't have an organization. We are simply men with families who . . .'

146

'Who prowl about in public places armed and ready to strike down police,' Kollberg snapped. 'Out with the names now.'

Ten minutes later he stowed the two family men into the back seat and drove them to Kungsholmsgatan, took the lift and pushed them inside Martin Beck's office.

'You'll be sorry for this as long as you live,' the elder man said.

'The only thing I'm sorry for is that I didn't break your arm,' Kollberg retorted.

Martin Beck gave him a quick, searching look and said:

'Okay, Lennart. You go home now.'

Kollberg went.

The man in the track suit opened his mouth to speak but Martin Beck checked him. He gestured to them to sit down, sat in silence for some moments with his elbows on the desk and pressed his palms together. Then he said:

'What you have done is indefensible. The very idea of militia comprises a far greater danger to society than any single criminal or gang. It paves the way for lynch mentality and arbitrary administration of justice. It throws the protective mechanism of society out of gear. Do you understand what I mean?'

'You're talking like a book,' said the man in the track suit acidly.

'Exactly,' Martin Beck replied. 'These are elementary facts. Mere catechism. Do you understand what I mean?'

It took about an hour before they understood what he meant.

When Kollberg got home to Palandergatan his wife was sitting up in bed knitting. Without saying a word he got undressed, went into the bathroom and had a shower. Then he got into bed. His wife put down her knitting and said:

'That's a nasty bruise on your neck. Has someone hit you?'

'Put your arms around me,' he said.

'My tummy's in the way, but . . . there. Who hit you?'

'A couple of damn amateurs,' Kollberg said and fell asleep.

22

At breakfast on Sunday morning Martin Beck's wife said:

'How are you doing? Can't you get hold of that creature? Look what happened to Lennart yesterday, it's awful. I don't wonder people are scared, but it's a bit much when they go for policemen.'

Martin Beck sat hunched over the table. He was wearing dressing gown and pyjamas. He was busy trying to recall a dream he had had just before waking up. An unpleasant dream. Something about Gunvald Larsson. Stubbing out the first cigarette of the day he looked at his wife.

'They didn't know he was a policeman,' he said.

'All the same,' she said. 'It's very nasty.'

'Yes. It's very nasty.'

She took a bite at a piece of toast and frowned at the stub in the ashtray.

'You shouldn't smoke so early in the morning. It's bad for your throat.'

'No,' Martin Beck said, withdrawing his hand from the pocket of the dressing gown.

He had been about to light another cigarette but now he left the packet where it was and thought: Inga's right. Of course

148

it's not good for me. I smoke far too much. And look what it costs.

'You smoke far too much,' she said. 'And look what it costs.'

'I know,' he said.

He wondered how many times she had said this during the sixteen years of their marriage. Even a guess seemed impossible.

'Are the children asleep?' he asked, changing the subject.

'Yes, it's the summer holiday. Our daughter was late getting home last night. I don't like her being out like that at night. Especially with that lunatic at large. She's only a child.'

'She will soon be sixteen,' he said. 'And from what I gathered she was with a friend next door.'

'Nilsson downstairs said yesterday that parents who let their children run about without keeping an eye on them have only themselves to blame. He said that there are minorities in the community – exhibitionists and the like – who have to get rid of their aggressions, and that it's the parents' fault if the children get into trouble.'

'Who's Nilsson?'

'The businessman who lives underneath us.'

'Has he children?'

'No.'

'Well then.'

'Just what I said. That he doesn't know what it is to have children. How worried one always is.'

'Why did you talk to him?'

'Well, you have to be nice to your neighbours. It wouldn't do any harm if you too were friendly to people sometimes. Anyway, they're very nice people.'

'It doesn't sound like it,' Martin Beck said.

Realizing that a quarrel was blowing up he quickly drained his cup of coffee.

'I must hurry and dress,' he said, getting up.

He went into the bedroom and sat down on the edge of the

bed. Inga washed up, and when he heard the water stop running and her footsteps approaching he retired swiftly into the bathroom and locked the door. Then he turned on the water, undressed and stretched out in the hot bath.

He lay quite still and relaxed. Closing his eyes, he tried to recall the dream he had had. He thought of Gunvald Larsson. Neither he nor Kollberg liked Gunvald Larsson, whom they only worked with sporadically, and he suspected that even Melander found it hard to appreciate this colleague, though he gave no sign of it. Gunvald Larsson had an unusual capacity to annoy Martin Beck, who felt irritated even now when he thought of him. But in some way he had a feeling that his present annoyance had nothing to do with Gunvald Larsson personally, but was rather something he had said or done. Martin Beck had an idea that Gunvald Larsson had said or done something important, something that was decisive for the park murders. Whatever it was eluded him, and it was no doubt this fact which was irritating him now.

He dismissed the thought and climbed out of the bath. It was probably all mixed up with his dream, he thought as he shaved.

A quarter of an hour later he was on his way into town on the underground. He opened his morning paper. On the front page was an identikit picture of the girls' murderer, drawn by the police artist from the meagre description given by witnesses, chiefly Rolf Evert Lundgren. Nobody was satisfied with it. Least of all the artist and Rolf Evert Lundgren.

Martin Beck held the paper away from him and looked at the picture with narrowed eyes. He wondered to what extent it really resembled the man they were hunting. They had also shown it to Mrs Engström, who at first had said it wasn't in the least like her dead husband but had then admitted there might be a resemblance.

Beneath the picture was the incomplete description. Martin Beck read the short text.

Suddenly he stiffened. Felt a wave of warmth pass through him.

Held his breath. In a flash he knew what it was that had been worrying him ever since they caught the mugger, what had niggled at him and what it was that linked up with Gunvald Larsson.

The description.

Gunvald Larsson's summary of the description Lundgren had given was almost word for word a repetition of something Martin Beck had heard him say on the phone over two weeks ago.

He remembered standing by the filing cabinet, listening to Gunvald Larsson speaking on the phone. Melander had also been in the room.

He could not recall the whole conversation, but seemed to remember that it had been with a woman who wanted to report a man who had been standing on a balcony in the block of flats opposite. Gunvald Larsson had asked her to describe the man and he had repeated the description in almost exactly the same words as Lundgren used when he was interrogated later. Also, the woman had said that the man kept watching children who were playing in the street.

Martin Beck folded up the paper and stared out of the window, trying to recall what had been said and done that morning. He knew on which day the conversation had taken place, for soon afterwards he had driven down to the Central Station and taken the train to Motala. It was Friday, 2 June, exactly a week before the murder in Vanadis Park.

He tried to remember whether the woman on the phone had given her address. Probably she had, and in that case Gunvald Larsson must have written it down somewhere.

As the train approached the city centre Martin Beck regarded this bright idea of his with waning enthusiasm. The description was so defective that it could fit thousands of people. The fact that Gunvald Larsson had used the same wording on two entirely different occasions need not mean that it referred to the same person. The fact that a man stands on his balcony at all times of the day and night need not mean that he is a presumptive murderer. The fact that Martin Beck on previous occasions had had a flash of intuition which had turned out to provide the solution to difficult cases need not mean that it would do so this time.

Still, it was worth looking into.

Usually he got off at T-Centralen and walked over the Klaraberg viaduct to Kungsholmsgatan, but today he took a taxi.

Gunvald Larsson was sitting at his desk drinking coffee, Kollberg half sat with one thigh over the edge of the desk, nibbling at a pastry. Martin Beck sat down in Melander's chair, stared at Gunvald Larsson and said:

'Do you remember that woman who called up the same day I went to Motala? She wanted to report a man who was standing on a balcony on the other side of the street?'

Kollberg put the rest of the pastry into his mouth and stared at Martin Beck in astonishment.

'Hell, yes,' Gunvald Larsson said. 'That loony bitch. What about her?'

'Do you remember how she described him?'

'No, I certainly don't. How can I remember what all these nutty people say?'

Kollberg swallowed with some difficulty and said:

'What are you talking about?'

Martin Beck waved him to be quiet and went on:

'Think hard, Gunvald. It might be important.'

Gunvald Larsson looked at him distrustfully.

'Why? Okay, wait, and I'll think.'

After a while he said:

'Now I've thought. No, I don't remember. I don't think there was anything special about him. He no doubt looked very ordinary.'

He shoved the knuckle of his first finger into a nostril and frowned.

'Wasn't his fly undone? No, wait . . . No, it was his shirt. He had a white shirt and it was unbuttoned. That's it, now I remember. The old woman said he had blue-grey eyes and then I asked how narrow the street was. And do you know what she said? That the street wasn't narrow at all but that she looked at him through binoculars. Crazy. She was a peeper, of course, and she's the one who ought to be locked up. Sitting gaping at men through binoculars . . .'

'What are you talking about?' Kollberg asked again.

'That's what I'm wondering,' Gunvald Larsson said. 'Why is that suddenly so important?'

Martin Beck sat silent for a moment. Then he said:

'I happened to think of that man on the balcony because Gunvald used the same wording when he repeated the woman's description as when he summed up Lundgren's description of the man in Vanadis Park. Thin hair brushed back, big nose, average height, white unbuttoned shirt, brown trousers, blue-grey eyes. Is that right?'

'Maybe,' Gunvald Larsson said. 'I don't really remember. But it fits Lundgren's man anyway.'

'You mean it could be the same person?' Kollberg asked doubtfully. 'It's not a very unusual description, is it?'

Martin Beck shrugged.

'No. It doesn't tell us very much. But ever since we questioned Lundgren I've had a hunch that there's a connection between the murders and that man on the balcony. It's just that I couldn't put my finger on it until today.'

He stroked his chin and looked awkwardly at Kollberg.

'It's a very frail supposition. Not much to go on. I know that. But it might be worth while checking up on that man.'

Kollberg got up and went over to the window. Stood with his back to it and folded his arms.

'Well, frail suppositions sometimes . . .'

Martin Beck was still looking at Gunvald Larsson.

'Come on now, try and remember that conversation. What did the woman say when she called?'

Gunvald Larsson flung out his big hands.

'That's all she said. That she wanted to report a man who was standing on the balcony opposite. She thought it funny.'

'Why did she think it funny?'

'Because he was nearly always standing there. At night too. She said she watched him through binoculars. That he stood looking down into the street at the cars and at children playing. Then she lost her temper because I was not sufficiently interested. But why should I be interested? People have a right to stand on their balconies without the neighbours calling up the police. Eh? What the hell did she want me to do?'

'Where did she live?' Martin Beck asked.

'I don't know,' Gunvald Larsson replied. 'I'm not even sure she said.'

'What was her name?' Kollberg asked.

'I don't know. Come to that, how the hell could I know?'

'Didn't you ask her?' Martin Beck said.

'Yes, I suppose I did. One always does.'

'Can't you remember?' Kollberg said. 'Think hard.'

Martin Beck and Kollberg watched with close attention the visible expressions of Gunvald Larsson's forced mental processes. He had his fair eyebrows drawn together so that they formed a continuous line above the clear blue eyes. He was also red in the face and looked as if he sat straining. After a while he said:

'No, I don't remember. Mrs . . . er . . . Mrs something.'

'Didn't you write it down anywhere?' Martin Beck asked. 'You always make a note of things.'

Gunvald Larsson glared at him.

'Yes, I do. But I don't keep all my notes. I mean, it wasn't anything important. A loony old girl calling up. Why should I remember it?'

Kollberg sighed.

154

'Well, where do we go from here?'

'When is Melander coming?' Martin Beck asked.

'Three o'clock, I think. He was working last night.'

'Call up and ask him to come here now,' Martin Beck said. 'He can sleep some other time.'

23

Sure enough, when Kollberg called up, Melander was asleep in his flat at the corner of Norr Mälarstrand and Polhemsgatan. Dressing at once, he drove the short distance to Kungsholmsgatan in his own car and only a quarter of an hour later he joined the other three.

He recalled the telephone conversation and when they had run the last part of the tape from the interrogation with Rolf Evert Lundgren, he confirmed that Martin Beck's theory concerning the description was correct. Then he asked for a cup of coffee and began carefully filling his pipe.

He lit up, leaned back in the chair and said:

'So you think there's some connection?'

'It's only supposition,' Martin Beck said. 'A contribution to the guessing competition.'

'There may be something in it, of course,' Melander said. 'What do you want me to do about it?'

'Use that built-in computer you have instead of a brain,' Kollberg said.

Melander nodded and went on calmly sucking at his pipe. Kollberg called him 'the living punch-card machine', which was a fitting name. Melander's memory had already become legendary within the force.

'Try and remember what Gunvald said and did when he got that phone call,' Martin Beck said.

'Wasn't it the day before Lennart came here?' Melander said. 'Let's see now . . . the second of June it must have been. I had the office next door then, and when Lennart came I moved in here.'

'Exactly,' Martin Beck said. 'And I went down to Motala that day. I was on the way to the train and only looked in to ask about that fence.'

'Larsson, the one who had died.'

Kollberg was perched on the window sill, listening. He had often been present when Melander recapitulated the course of events – sometimes they had been much farther back than this – and he always had the feeling that he was witnessing a séance.

Melander had taken up what Kollberg called 'his thinker pose': he was leaning back in the chair with his legs stretched full length but crossed, his eyes half shut, and drawing calmly at his pipe. Martin Beck, as usual, stood with one arm on the filing cabinet.

'When I came in you were standing exactly where you're standing now and Gunvald sat where he's sitting now. We were talking about that fence when the phone rang. Gunvald answered. He said his name and asked hers, I remember that.'

'Do you remember whether he wrote the name down?' Martin Beck asked.

'I think so. I remember he had a pen in his hand. Yes, he must have made a note of it.'

'Do you remember whether he asked for the address?'

'No, I don't think he did. But she may have given both name and address all at once.'

Martin Beck looked inquiringly at Gunvald Larsson, who shrugged.

'I don't recall any address at any rate,' he said.

'Then he said something about a cat,' Melander said.

'So I did,' Gunvald Larsson said. 'I thought that's what she said. That there was a cat on her balcony. Then she said it was a man and of course I thought she meant that he was standing on *her* balcony. Seeing as she called the police.'

'Then you asked her to describe the man and I remember plainly that you made notes at the same time as you repeated what she said.'

'Okay,' Gunvald Larsson said, 'but if I made notes, which I've no doubt I did, then I wrote on the block here, and since it turned out that no action was needed, I probably tore the sheet off and threw it away.'

Martin Beck lit a cigarette, walked over and put the match in Melander's ashtray and returned to his place at the cabinet.

'Yes, I'm afraid you probably did,' he said. 'Go on, Fredrik.'

'It wasn't until after she'd given you the description that you realized he was standing on his own balcony, eh?'

'Yes,' Gunvald Larsson said. 'I thought the old girl was nutty.'

'Then you asked how it was she could see that he had blue-grey eyes if he was on the other side of the street.'

'That was when the old girl said she had been watching him through binoculars.'

Melander looked up in surprise.

'Binoculars? Good Lord.'

'Yes, and I asked if he had molested her in any way, but he hadn't. He just stood there, and she thought it was nasty, she said.'

'He evidently stood there at night too,' Melander said.

'Yes. That's what she said anyway.'

'And you asked what he was looking at and she said that he kept looking down at the street. At cars and children playing. And then you asked if she thought you ought to send the dog van.'

Gunvald Larsson looked irritably at Martin Beck and said:

'Yes, Martin had been standing here nagging about it. It was a good chance for him to send out his damn dog van.'

Martin Beck exchanged a glance with Kollberg but said nothing.

'That was the end of the conversation, I think,' Melander said. 'The old girl thought you were insolent and put down the phone. And I went back to my room.'

Martin Beck sighed.

'Well, that's not much to go on. Except that the description tallies.'

'Funny for a guy to stand on his balcony day and night,' Kollberg said. 'Maybe he'd been pensioned off and had nothing else to do.'

'No,' Gunvald Larsson said. 'It wasn't that . . . Now I remember she said "And he's a young man too. Couldn't be over forty. Seems to have nothing better to do than stand there staring." Those were her very words. I'd quite forgotten.'

Martin Beck lowered his arm from the cabinet and said:

'In that case it also fits Lundgren's description. About forty. If she examined him in the binoculars she should have seen him pretty plainly.'

'Didn't she say how long she'd been looking at him before she called you up?' Kollberg asked.

Gunvald Larsson thought hard for a moment, then said:

'Wait now . . . Yes, she said she had been observing him for the last two months but that he might easily have been there earlier without her thinking anything of it. First she'd thought he stood debating whether to take his life or not. To jump, she said.'

'Are you sure you still haven't your notes somewhere?' Martin Beck asked.

Gunvald Larsson pulled out a drawer, took out a thin bundle of papers of different sizes, laid them in front of him and started looking through them.

'These are all the notes about things that have to be followed up and reported on. When the matter has been dealt with I throw the notes away,' he said as he fingered through them.

Melander leaned forward and knocked out his pipe.

'Yes,' he said. 'You had the pen in your hand and as you picked up the note pad you moved the telephone directory aside . . .'

Gunvald Larsson had looked through the bundle and put it back in the drawer.

'No, I know I haven't kept any notes of that conversation. It's a pity, but I haven't.'

Melander raised his pipe and pointed at Gunvald Larsson with the stem.

'The telephone directory,' he said.

'What telephone directory?'

'A telephone directory was lying open on your desk. Didn't you write in that?'

'It's possible.'

Gunvald Larsson reached for his telephone directories and said:

'Hell of a job looking through all these.'

Putting down his pipe, Melander said:

'You don't have to. If you wrote anything – and I think you did – it wasn't in your directory.'

Martin Beck suddenly saw the scene in front of him. Melander had come into the room from next door with an open telephone directory in his hands, given it to him and shown him the name of the fence, Arvid Larsson. Then Martin Beck himself had put the directory down on the desk.

'Lennart,' he said. 'Would you mind getting the first part of the telephone directory in your room?'

Martin Beck looked first for the page giving *Larsson Arvid sec. hand furn.* No notes there. Then he started at the beginning and looked through the directory carefully page by page. In several places he found illegible scrawls, most of them written in Melander's unmistakable hand but also some in Kollberg's clear and legible writing. The others stood round him in silence, waiting. Gunvald Larsson looked over his shoulder.

Not until he got to page 1082 did Gunvald Larsson exclaim:
'There!'
All four of them stared at the note in the margin.
A single word.
Andersson.

24

Andersson.

Gunvald Larsson put his head on one side and looked at the name.

'Yes, it looks like Andersson all right. Or maybe Andersen. Or Andresen. It might be damn anything. Though I think it's meant to be Andersson.'

Andersson.

There are three hundred and ninety thousand people in Sweden called Andersson. The Stockholm telephone directory alone lists ten thousand two hundred subscribers with this name, plus another two thousand in the immediate environs.

Martin Beck thought this over. It might turn out to be very easy to get hold of the woman who had made the much-discussed phone call, provided they made use of press, radio and television. But it could also be very difficult. And up to now nothing had been easy during this investigation.

They did make use of press, radio and television.

Nothing happened.

It was understandable that nothing happened on Sunday.

By eleven o'clock on Monday morning there were still no developments and Martin Beck began to have his doubts.

To start door-to-door questioning and calling up thousands of subscribers meant that a very great part of the search squad must be freed from other work to follow up a clue which might very well turn out to be useless. But couldn't the sphere of work be limited in some way? A rather wide street. It must be somewhere in the central part of the city.

'Must it?' Kollberg said doubtfully.

'Of course not, but ...'

'But what? Is your intuition telling you something?'

Martin Beck gave him a harried look, then pulled himself together and said:

'The underground ticket, which was bought at Rådmansgatan.'

'And which is not proved to have any connection with either the murders or the murderer,' Kollberg said.

'It was bought at the station at Rådmansgatan and used only in one direction,' Martin Beck said obstinately. 'The murderer kept it because he intended using it for the return journey. He took the subway from Rådmansgatan to Mariatorget or Zinkensdamm and walked the rest of the way to Tanto Park.'

'Mere speculation,' Kollberg said.

'He had to do something to get rid of the little boy who was with the girl. He had nothing else to hand but the ticket.'

'Speculation,' Kollberg said.

'But it sticks together logically.'

'Only just.'

'And besides, the first murder was committed in Vanadis Park. It's all linked up with that part of the city. Vanadis Park, Rådmansgatan, the whole area north of Odengatan.'

'You've said that before,' Kollberg said drily. 'It's pure guess-work.'

'The theory of probability.'

'You can call it that too if you like.'

'I want to get hold of that Andersson woman,' Martin Beck said, 'and we can't just sit twiddling our thumbs and wait for her to come to us of her own accord. She may not have a TV, she may not read the papers. But she must have a telephone at any rate.'

'Must she?'

'Without a doubt. You don't make a call like that from a phone box or a tobacconist's. Besides, it seemed as if she was watching the man while she talked.'

'Okay, I give in on that point.'

'And if we're going to start ringing around and go from door to door, we must begin somewhere, within a certain area. Seeing that we haven't enough men in the force to contact every single person by the name of Andersson.'

Kollberg sat in silence for a while. Then he said:

'Let's leave this Andersson woman for a moment and ask ourselves instead what we know of the murderer.'

'We have a sort of description.'

'Sort of, yes, that just about sums it up. And we don't know if it *was* the murderer Lundgren saw, if indeed he saw anyone.'

'We know it's a man.'

'Yes. What else do we know?'

'We know that he's not in the vice squad's records.'

'Yes. Provided no one has been careless or forgotten something. That has happened before.'

'We know the approximate times the murders were committed – soon after seven in the evening in Vanadis Park and between two and three in the afternoon in Tanto. So he wasn't at work then.'

'Which implies?'

Martin Beck said nothing. Kollberg answered his own question:

'That he's out of work, is on holiday, is on sick leave, is only visiting Stockholm, has irregular working hours, is pensioned off, is a vagrant or . . . in short, it implies nothing at all.'

'True enough,' Martin Beck said. 'But we do have some idea of his behaviour pattern.'

'You mean the psychologists' rigmarole?'

'Yes.'

'That's only guesswork too, but . . .'

Kollberg was silent for a moment before going on:

'But I must admit that Melander made a very plausible extract from all that stuff.'

'Yes.'

'As for this woman and her phone call, let's try and find her. And since we must start somewhere, as you so aptly pointed out, and since we're only guessing our way along anyway, we might just as well presume that you are right. How do you want it done?'

'We'll start in the fifth and ninth districts,' Martin Beck said. 'Put a couple of men on to calling up everyone by the name of Andersson and a couple more on to door knocking. We'll ask the entire personnel in those districts to focus their attention on this particular question. Especially along wide streets where there are balconies – Odengatan, Karlbergsvägen, Tegnérgatan, Sveavägen and so on.'

'Okay,' Kollberg said.

They set to work.

It was an awful Monday. The Great Detective (the general public), who had seemed less busy during Sunday, partly because so many people had gone to the country for the weekend, partly because of the reassuring appeals in press and television, were fully active once more. The central office for tips was swamped with calls from people who thought they knew something, from lunatics who wanted to confess and from scoundrels who called up just to be sworn at. Parks and wooded areas swarmed with plainclothes police, as far as a hundred men can be said to swarm, and on top of all this came the search for someone called Andersson.

And the whole time fear was lurking in the background. Many parents called the police about children who had not been away from home for longer than fifteen or twenty minutes. Everything had to be noted down and checked. The material grew and grew. And in all cases was utterly useless.

In the middle of all this Hansson in fifth district called up.

'Have you found another body?' Martin Beck said.

'No, but I'm worried about that Eriksson we were to keep an eye on. The exhibitionist you had in custody.'

'What about him?'

'He hasn't been out since last Wednesday, when he brought home a lot of drink, mostly wine. He went from one off licence to another.'

'And then?'

'We caught a glimpse of him now and again in the window. He looked like a ghost, the boys said. But there hasn't been a sign of him since yesterday morning.'

'Have you rung the doorbell?'

'Yes. He won't open the door.'

Martin Beck had almost forgotten the man. Now he remembered the furtive, miserable eyes, the trembling, emaciated hands. He felt a chill spread over his body.

'Break in,' he said.

'How?'

'Any way you like.'

Putting down the phone, he sat with his head in his hands. No, he thought, not this on top of everything else.

Half an hour later Hansson called up again.

'He had turned the gas on.'

'And?'

'He's on the way to hospital now. Alive.'

Martin Beck sighed. With relief, as they say.

'Though only just,' Hansson said. 'He had done it very neatly. Sealed up the cracks around the doors and stuffed up the keyholes of both front door and kitchen door.'

'But he'll be all right?'

'Yes, thanks to the usual. The tokens in the meter gave out. But if he'd been left to lie there any longer . . .'

Hansson left the rest of the sentence unsaid.

'Had he written anything?'

'Yes. "I can't go on". He had scrawled it on the edge of an old girlie magazine. I've notified the temperance board.'

'It should have been done before.'

'Well, he did his job all right,' Hansson replied.

After a moment or two he added:

'Until you picked him up.'

Several hours of this horrible Monday still remained. At about eleven in the evening Martin Beck and Kollberg went home. Gunvald Larsson too. Melander stayed on. Everyone knew that he loathed having to be up all night and that the mere thought of giving up his ten hours' sleep was a nightmare to him, but he himself said nothing and his expression was as stoical as ever.

Nothing had happened. Many women called Andersson had been interviewed, but none of them had made the now-famous phone call.

No more bodies had been found and all the children reported missing during the day had turned up safely.

Martin Beck walked to Fridhemsplan and took the underground home.

They had got through the day. It was over a week now since the last murder. Or rather the latest one.

He felt like a drowning man who has just found a foothold but who knows that it's only a respite. That in a few hours it will be high tide.

25

It was early in the morning of Tuesday 20 June and in the guard-room of ninth district police station things were still quiet. Police Officer Kvist sat at a table smoking and reading the paper. He was a young man with a fair beard. From behind the partition in the corner came the murmur of voices, interrupted now and then by the clatter of a typewriter. A telephone rang. Kvist looked up from his paper and saw Granlund lift the receiver inside the glass cage.

The door behind him opened and Rodin came in. He stopped inside the door and fastened his belt and shoulder strap. He was a good bit older than Kvist, both in years and length of service. Kvist had finished his training at the police school the year before and been transferred to ninth district quite recently.

Rodin went up to the table and picked up his cap. He slapped Kvist on the shoulder.

'Well, mate, let's go. We'll do one more round, then have coffee.'

Kvist stubbed out his cigarette and folded up the paper.

They went out of the main door and started walking westwards along Surbrunnsgatan. Slowly side by side, with equally long steps and hands behind their backs.

'What was it Granlund said we were to do with that Andersson woman if we found her?' Kvist asked.

'Nothing. Ask if she was the one who called up headquarters on the second of June and blethered about a man on a balcony,' Rodin said. 'Then we were to call Granlund.'

They passed Tulegatan and Kvist looked up towards Vanadis Park.

'Were you up there after the murder?' he asked.

'Yes,' Rodin said. 'Weren't you?'

'No, it was my day off.'

They walked on in silence. Then Kvist said:

'I've never found a body. It must have looked horrible.'

'Don't worry, you'll see a lot of them before you're through.'

'What made you join the police?' Kvist asked.

Rodin did not answer at once. Seemed to think it over. Then he said:

'My dad was a policeman. It seemed natural for me to be one too, though Mum wasn't too happy about it, of course. And you? What made you want to be a cop?'

'To do something for the good of the community,' Kvist said.

He gave a laugh and went on:

'At first I didn't know what I wanted to do. I had only Bs in my school-leaving certificate, but I met a guy in the army when I was doing my national service who was going to be a policeman and he said that my grades were good enough to get me into the police school. Also, there's a shortage of men in the force and . . . well, anyway, he talked me into it.'

'The pay's pretty lousy,' Rodin said.

'Oh, I dunno,' Kvist said. 'I got fourteen hundred kronor a month training pay and now I'm up in the ninth salary grade.'

'Yes, it's a bit better now than when I started.'

'I read somewhere,' Kvist said, 'that the police force is recruited out of the twenty per cent that does not go to trade schools or university, and that many of that twenty per cent do as you did, take the same job as their fathers. It just so happened that your father was a policeman.'

'Yes. But I damn well wouldn't have taken the same job if he'd been a dustman,' Rodin said.

'They say that there are at least fifteen hundred jobs vacant all over the country,' Kvist said. 'So, no wonder we have to do so much overtime.'

Rodin kicked aside an empty beer can lying on the pavement and said:

'You certainly are up on statistics. Do you intend to become commissioner?'

Kvist laughed, slightly embarrassed.

'Oh, I just read an article about it. But maybe it's not a bad idea to be commissioner. What do you think he earns?'

'Well, you ought to know, with all your reading.'

They had reached Sveavägen and the conversation flagged.

By the news kiosk at the corner, outside the off licence, stood a couple of distinctly drunken men, pushing each other. One of them kept shaking his fist and trying to strike the second man, but was evidently too drunk to succeed. The other man appeared slightly more sober and kept his antagonist at bay by pushing the flat of his hand against his chest. At last the more sober of the men lost patience and tumbled the spluttering troublemaker into the gutter.

Rodin sighed.

'We'll have to take him with us,' he said, starting to cross the road. 'I know him of old, he's always making trouble.'

'Which one?' Kvist asked.

'The one in the gutter. The other can manage on his own.'

They strode quickly up to the men. A third and equally seedy-looking type who had been watching the altercation from the small garden outside the Metropole restaurant moved off towards Odengatan with hard-won dignity, looking back anxiously over his shoulder.

The two policemen lifted the drunk out of the gutter and stood him on his feet. He was in his sixties, very lean and very underweight by the look of him. Several passers-by, classed as ordinary decent citizens, stopped at a distance and gaped.

'Well, Johansson, how are things today?' Rodin said.

Johansson's head flopped and he made a feeble attempt to dust himself down.

'Jush f-fine, offisher. I was jush talking to my mate here, jush having a bit of f-fun, shee?'

His friend made a commendable attempt to straighten up and said:

'Nothing wrong with Oskar. He'll be all right.'

'Scram,' Rodin said good-naturedly, waving him away.

Relieved, the man hurried out of harm's way.

Rodin and Kvist took a firm grip under the drunk's arms and started hauling him towards the taxi stand twenty yards farther off.

The taxi driver saw them coming, got out and opened the door to the back seat. He was one of the cooperative types.

'You're going to have a ride in a taxi, Johansson,' Rodin said. 'And then you can sleep.'

Johansson crawled meekly into the taxi, collapsed on the back seat and fell asleep. Rodin propped him up in the corner and said over his shoulder to Kvist:

'I'll book him and see you at the station. Buy a few cakes on the way back.'

Kvist nodded and as the taxi swung out from the kerb he walked slowly back to the news kiosk at the corner. He looked around for Johansson's mate and discovered him in Surbrunnsgatan, a few yards away from the off licence. When Kvist took a couple of steps towards him the man waved him away with both hands and started walking up towards Hagagatan.

Kvist watched the man until he had disappeared around the corner. Then he turned on his heel and returned to Sveavägen.

The saleswoman in the news kiosk stuck her head out of the opening and said:

'Thank you. Those drunks ruin my business. And they're always hanging about just here.'

'It's the off licence that attracts them,' Kvist said.

In a way he felt sorry for Johansson and his like, knowing that part of their trouble was that they had nowhere to spend their time.

He saluted and walked on. A little farther down Sveavägen he saw a shop sign: BAKERY. Looking at his watch, he thought he might as well buy the cakes there and go back to the station and have coffee.

A little bell tinkled as he opened the door of the bakery. An elderly woman in a checked smock stood at the counter talking to the woman who was serving her.

Kvist put his hands behind his back and waited. He inhaled the smell of fresh-baked bread, thinking that these small bakeries were getting rare.

Soon they'll vanish altogether and you'll be able to buy nothing but mass-produced bread in plastic wrapping and the entire Swedish nation will eat exactly the same loaves and buns and cakes, thought Police Officer Kvist.

Kvist was only twenty-two but often had the feeling that his childhood was in the distant past. He listened with half an ear to the conversation between the two women.

'And to think old Palm in Number 81 went and died,' said the fat woman in the smock.

'Yes, but just as well he did really,' the shopwoman said. 'He was so old and decrepit.'

She was grey-haired and elderly and wore a white coat. Casting a glance at Kvist, she quickly put the goods into the customer's shopping bag.

'Will that be all, Mrs Andersson?' she asked. 'No cream today?'

The customer picked up her bag and puffed.

'No, no cream today, thank you. And charge it as usual, please. Good morning.'

She moved towards the door and Kvist hurried to open it for her.

'Good morning, Mrs Andersson, dear,' the shopkeeper said.

The fat woman squeezed past Kvist with a nod by way of thanks.

He smiled to himself at the 'dear' and was about to close the door behind her when a thought struck him. The shopkeeper stared at him blankly as, without saying a word, he hurried out into the street and shut the door behind him.

As he caught up with her the woman in the check smock was already halfway inside the entrance next to the bakery. Saluting quickly, he said:

'Excuse me, madam, is your name Andersson?'

'Ye-es . . . ?'

Taking her shopping bag, he held open the door for her. When it had shut behind them he said:

'Forgive my asking, but was it by any chance you who called police headquarters on the morning of Friday the second of June?'

'The second of June? Ye-es, I did call the police. Maybe it was the second. What of it?'

'Why did you make that call?' Kvist asked.

He could not help betraying his eagerness and the woman called Andersson looked at him in astonishment.

'I spoke to a detective or whatever he was. A very rude man. Didn't seem in the least interested. I only wanted to report something I'd noticed. That man had been standing there on his balcony for . . .'

'Do you mind if I come up with you and use your phone?' Kvist asked, already on his way to the lift.

'I'll explain on the way up,' he said.

26

Martin Beck put down the phone and shouted to Kollberg. Then he buttoned his jacket, put his cigarettes and a box of matches in his pocket and looked at his wrist watch. Five to ten. Kollberg appeared in the doorway.

'What are you bawling for?' he said.

'They've found her. Mrs Andersson. Granlund in ninth district just called up. She lives in Sveavägen.'

Kollberg vanished into the next room, fetched his jacket and was still struggling into it when he came back.

'Sveavägen,' he said thoughtfully, looking at Martin Beck. 'How did they get hold of her? Door-to-door?'

'No, a young officer from ninth met her in a bakery when he went in to buy cakes.'

As they went downstairs Kollberg said:

'Isn't it Granlund who says that coffee breaks should be abolished? Perhaps he'll change his mind now.'

Mrs Andersson regarded them critically through the crack in the door.

'Was it either of you I spoke to when I called that morning?' she asked.

'No,' Martin Beck said politely. 'You spoke to Detective Inspector Larsson.'

Mrs Andersson undid the safety chain and admitted them to a small, dark hall.

'Detective inspector or not, he was very rude. As I said to the young officer who came up with me, the police ought to be grateful that people do report things. Who knows, I said to him, if people didn't report things you might not have any work. But step inside, please, and I'll get the coffee.'

Kollberg and Martin Beck went into the living room. Even though the flat was on the third floor and the window gave on to the street, the room was rather dark. It was large, but the heavy, old furniture took up most of the floor space. One half of the window was slightly open, the other half mostly hidden by tall pot plants. The curtains were cream-coloured and fussily draped.

In front of a brown plush sofa stood a round mahogany table set with coffee cups and a plate of cakes. Two tall armchairs with antimacassars stood one on each side of the table.

Mrs Andersson came in from the kitchen carrying a china coffeepot. She poured out the coffee and then sat down on the sofa, which groaned beneath her weight.

'Can't talk without coffee,' she said cheerfully. 'Do tell me now, has anything happened about that man opposite?'

Martin Beck started to say something but his words were drowned by the wail of an ambulance tearing along the street below. Kollberg closed the window.

'Haven't you read the papers, Mrs Andersson?' Martin Beck asked.

'No, when I'm in the country I never read the papers. I came home last night. Have another cake, gentlemen. Go on, do, they're just fresh from the bakery downstairs. By the way, that's where I met that nice young man in uniform, though how he could know *I* was the one to call up the police, I'm sure I don't know. Anyway,

I did and it was the second of June, a Friday, I remember quite well, because my sister's husband's name is Rutger and it was his name day, and when I was there with them at the coffee party I told them about that rude inspector or whatever he was and it was only an hour or two after I had called up.'

Here she had to get her breath and Martin Beck put in quickly: 'Would you mind showing us that balcony?'

Kollberg had already gone over to the window. The woman heaved herself up.

'The third balcony from the bottom,' she said, pointing. 'Beside that window with no curtains.'

They looked at the balcony. The flat to which it belonged seemed to have only two windows on to the street, a large one near the balcony door and a smaller one.

'Have you seen the man recently?' Martin Beck asked.

'No, not for some time. You see, I was in the country over the weekend, but before that I didn't see him for some days.'

Kollberg caught sight of a pair of binoculars between two flower pots on the window sill. He picked them up and looked through them at the flat opposite. The balcony door and the windows were shut. The windowpanes reflected the daylight and he could not make out anything inside the dark rooms.

'Rutger gave me those binoculars,' the woman said. 'They're naval ones. Rutger used to be a naval officer. I usually look at that man through the binoculars. If you open the window you can see better. Don't go thinking I'm inquisitive, now, but you see I had an operation on my leg at the beginning of April and that was when I discovered that man. After the operation, that is. I had this incision in my leg and I couldn't walk and it hurt so much I couldn't sleep either, so I sat here at the window most of the time, watching. I thought there was something very peculiar about a man who had nothing better to do than stand there staring. Ugh. There was something nasty about him.'

While the woman was talking Martin Beck took out the identikit picture that had been drawn from the mugger's description and showed it to her.

'Quite like him,' she said. 'Not very well drawn, if you ask me. But there's a likeness all right.'

'Do you remember when you saw him last?' Kollberg asked, handing the binoculars to Martin Beck.

'Well, it's some days ago now. Over a week. Let's see now ... yes, I think the last time was when I had the woman in to clean. Wait and I'll have a look.'

Opening the writing desk, she took out a calendar.

'Let's see now ... Last Friday, that's it. We cleaned the windows. He was standing there in the morning but not in the evening and not the next day. Yes, that's right. Since then I haven't seen him. I'm sure of that.'

Martin Beck lowered the binoculars and glanced swiftly at Kollberg. They didn't need a calendar to remember what had happened on that Friday.

'On the ninth, that is,' Kollberg said.

'That's right. Now what about another cup of coffee?'

'No, thank you,' Martin Beck said.

'Oh, just a drop, come on.'

'No, thank you,' Kollberg said.

She filled the cups and sank down on to the sofa. Kollberg perched on the arm of the chair and popped a small almond biscuit into his mouth.

'Was he always alone, that man?' Martin Beck asked.

'Well, I've never seen anyone else there at any rate. He looks the lonely type. Sometimes I almost feel sorry for him. It's always dark in the apartment and when he's not standing on the balcony he sits at the kitchen window. He does that when it rains. But I've never seen anyone with him. But do sit down and have some more coffee and tell me what's happened to him. Just think, my calling up did the trick after all. But it took an awfully long time.'

Martin Beck and Kollberg had already gulped down their coffee. They stood up.

'Thanks very much, Mrs Andersson. Good-bye. No, please don't bother to see us out.'

They retreated towards the hall.

When they came out of the main entrance Kollberg, law-abiding, started walking towards the pedestrian crossing fifty yards away, but Martin Beck took him by the arm and they hurried across the road towards the block of flats on the other side.

27

Martin Beck walked up the three flights, Kollberg took the lift. They met outside the door and looked at it attentively. An ordinary brown wooden door that opened inwards, with Yale lock, brass letter box and a tarnished white-metal nameplate, on which was engraved in black letters: I. FRANSSON. There was not a sound in the whole building. Kollberg put his right ear to the door and listened. Then he knelt down with his right knee on the stone floor and very cautiously pushed up the flap of the letter box about half an inch. Listened. Lowered the flap as silently as he had raised it. Got up and shook his head.

Martin Beck shrugged, stretched out his right hand and pressed the button of the electric doorbell. Not a sound. The bell was evidently out of order. He tapped on the door. No result. Kollberg pounded with his fist. Nothing happened.

They did not open the door themselves. They went downstairs half a flight and spoke in whispers. Then Kollberg went off to arrange the formalities and send for an expert. Martin Beck remained standing on the stairs and never took his eyes off the door.

After only a quarter of an hour Kollberg returned with the expert, who sized up the door with a quick, trained glance, dropped to his knees and stuck a long but handy instrument like a pair of tongs through the letter box. The lock had no antiburglar device over it on the inside and he needed only thirty seconds to grip it and work open the door a few inches. Martin Beck pushed past him and put his left index finger against the door. Opened it. The unoiled hinges creaked.

They looked into a hall with two open doors. The left one led into the kitchen and the right one into what was apparently the only room in the flat. A pile of post lay on the doormat, so far as they could see chiefly newspapers, advertisements and brochures. The bathroom lay to the right of the hall, just inside the front door.

The only sound was the muffled roar of traffic from Sveavägen.

Martin Beck and Kollberg stepped carefully over the pile of post and glanced into the kitchen. At the far end was a small dining area with a window on to the street.

Kollberg pushed open the door of the bathroom while Martin Beck went into the living room. Straight in front of him was the balcony door and obliquely behind him to the right he saw another door, which he found led into a wardrobe. Kollberg said a few words to the lock expert, closed the front door and came into the room.

'Obviously no one at home,' he said.

'No,' Martin Beck said.

They went through the flat systematically but with great caution, taking care to touch as few objects as possible.

The windows, one in the living room and one in the dining area, gave on to the street and were shut; so was the balcony door. The air was close and stale.

The flat was in no way dilapidated or neglected, yet somehow it seemed shabby. It was also very bare. The living room had only three pieces of furniture: an unmade bed with a torn, red quilt and grubby sheets, a kitchen chair at the head of the bed and, by the opposite wall, a low chest of drawers. No curtains and no rug on the linoleum floor. On the chair, which evidently served as a bedside table, lay a box of matches, a saucer and an issue of the *Småland Gazette*. The newspaper was folded up in a way that indicated it had been read, and on the saucer lay a little tobacco ash, seven dead matches and small, tight balls of cigarette paper.

Above the chest of drawers hung a framed reproduction of an oil painting of two horses and a birch tree, and on the chest of drawers stood another ornament, a glazed blue ceramic dish. Empty. That was all.

Kollberg regarded the objects on the chair and said:

'Looks as if he saves the tobacco from the cigarette butts and smokes it in a pipe.'

Martin Beck nodded.

They didn't go out on to the balcony but merely looked through the glass pane of the closed door. The balcony had an iron tube railing and the sides were of corrugated iron. It was furnished with a rickety varnished garden table and a folding chair. The chair looked old, with worn wooden arms and faded canvas seat.

In the closet hung a reasonably good dark-blue suit, a threadbare winter overcoat and a pair of brown corduroy trousers. On the shelf lay a fur cap and a woollen scarf and on the floor one black shoe and a pair of worn-out brown boots. They looked about size 8.

'Small feet,' Kollberg said. 'Wonder where the other shoe is.'

They found it a few minutes later in the broom cupboard. Beside it lay a cleaning rag and a shoe brush. The shoe looked to be smeared with something, but the light was bad and they didn't want to touch it; they just stared into the dark cupboard.

The kitchen offered several other things of interest. On the gas cooker was a large box of matches and a saucepan with remains of food. Looked like oatmeal, quite dried up. On the sink an enamel coffeepot and a dirty cup with a thin layer of dregs in the bottom. Dry as dust. Also a soup plate and a can of coarse-ground coffee. Along the other wall was a refrigerator and two kitchen cupboards with sliding doors. The men opened all three. The refrigerator contained an opened half-packet of margarine, two eggs and a bit of sausage, which was so old that it was covered with a thin layer of mould.

One of the cupboards seemed to be used for china, the other as a pantry. A few plates, cups and glasses, a serving dish, salt, half a loaf of bread, a packet of sugar lumps and a bag of rolled oats. In the drawers underneath were a carving knife and several odd knives, forks and spoons.

Kollberg poked at the bread. It was hard as a stone.

'He doesn't seem to have been home for a while,' he said.

'No,' Martin Beck agreed.

In the cupboard under the draining board was a frying pan and saucepans and in the opening under the sink was a bin liner. It was almost empty.

By the window in the dining recess stood a red kitchen table with leaves and two kitchen chairs. On the table stood two bottles and a dirty glass. The bottles had contained ordinary sweet vermouth. One of them still had a little in the bottom.

Both window sill and table top were covered with a film of greasy dirt, obviously exhaust fumes from the street, which had seeped in through the cracks of the window, although this was shut.

Kollberg went into the bathroom and had a look, returned after half a minute and shook his head.

'Nothing there.'

The two top drawers of the chest of drawers contained shirts, a cardigan, socks, underclothes and two ties. They all seemed clean but threadbare. The bottom drawer was full of dirty linen. There was also an enrolment book from the army.

They opened it and read: *2521-7-46 Fransson Ingemund Rudolf Växjö 5/2–26 Gardener Västergatan 22 Malmö.*

Martin Beck leafed through the enrolment book. It told him quite a lot about what Ingemund Rudolf Fransson had been doing up to and including the year 1947. He was born in Småland forty-one years ago. In 1946 he had had a job as a gardening labourer in Malmö and had lived in Västergatan there. In the same year he had been called up, had been graded as C3 and unfit for armed service, and had served twelve months with the anti-aircraft regiment in Malmö. On being discharged from the army in 1947 someone with an illegible signature had given him the rating X-5-5, which lay well below average. The Roman figure was a mark of military conduct and showed that he had not been guilty of any breach of discipline, the two fives indicated that he was not much of a soldier, even within the C3 category. The officer with the illegible signature had given him the laconic utility code 'kitchen hand', which probably meant that he had performed his national service peeling potatoes.

Otherwise their rapid and superficial search of the flat revealed nothing about Ingemund Fransson's present occupation or about his doings during the last twenty years.

'The post,' Kollberg said, going out into the hall.

Martin Beck nodded. He was standing by the bed, looking down at it. The sheets were crumpled and grubby, the pillow squashed into a lump. Even so, it didn't look as if anyone had slept in it for several days.

Kollberg came back.

'Only newspapers and advertisements,' he said. 'What's the date of the paper lying there?'

Martin Beck put his head on one side, narrowed his eyes and said:

'Thursday the eighth of June.'

'It evidently comes the day after. He hasn't touched his post since Saturday the tenth. Not after the murder in Vanadis Park.'

'Yet he seems to have been home on Monday.'

'Yes,' Kollberg agreed, then added:

'But hardly since then.'

Martin Beck stretched out his right arm, took hold of one

corner of the pillowcase with thumb and forefinger and lifted the pillow.

Under it lay two pairs of little girls' white panties.

Seemed very small.

Stained by spots in different shades.

They stood quite still in the stale, bleak room, listening to the traffic and their own breathing. For perhaps twenty seconds. Then Martin Beck said swiftly and tonelessly:

'Okay. That's it. We'll seal off the flat and alert the technical squad.'

'Pity there was no photograph,' Kollberg said.

Martin Beck thought of the dead man in the condemned house in Västmannagatan who had not yet been identified. It could be the same one but it was far from certain. Not even likely.

They still knew very little about the man called Ingemund Fransson.

Three hours later the time was two o'clock in the afternoon of Tuesday, 20 June, and they knew considerably more.

For one thing, the dead man in Västmannagatan was not identical with Ingemund Fransson. Several nauseated witnesses had confirmed this.

The police had at last got hold of a loose end of thread, and with the aid of the well-oiled and ruthlessly efficient investigation machinery they soon unravelled the relatively simple tangle concerning Ingemund Fransson's past. They had already been in touch with about a hundred persons: neighbours, shopkeepers, social workers, doctors, army officers, clergymen, temperance administrators and many others. The picture cleared up very quickly.

Ingemund Fransson had moved to Malmö in 1943 and had got a job with the parks branch of the municipal council. His change of domicile was probably due to the fact that he had lost his parents. His father, who had been a labourer in Växjö, had died in the spring and his mother had already been dead for five years. He had no other relations. As soon as he had done his national service he had moved to Stockholm. He had lived in the flat in Sveavägen since 1948 and had been employed as a gardening labourer until 1956. He then gave up his job, was sick-listed first by a doctor in private practice, then gradually examined by various psychiatrists in social welfare and was finally pensioned off two years later as unfit to work. The official report had the somewhat mystifying wording: 'mentally incapable of physical work'.

The doctors concerned said that he had more than average talent but was seized by a kind of chronic fear of work which simply prevented him from going off to work. Attempts at rehabilitation had failed. When he was supposed to be working in a machine shop he went to the factory gates every morning for four weeks but could not bring himself to go in. It was said that this type of inability to work was rare but by no means unique. Fransson was not mentally ill in any way or in need of care. There was nothing wrong with his intelligence and he had no physical defects to speak of. (The army doctor had given him a low rating because of flat feet.) But he was very unsociable, had no need of human contact, no friends and no interests, apart from what a doctor called 'a vague interest in his native Småland countryside'. He had a quiet, friendly manner, did not drink, was extremely economical and could be considered orderly, although he 'didn't bother much about his appearance'. He smoked. No sexual abnormalities had been apparent; Fransson had answered very vaguely when asked whether he was in the habit of masturbating, but the doctor presumed that he did so and that in any case he had an unusually weak sex urge. He suffered from agoraphobia.

Most of this dated from doctors' reports of the years 1957 and 1958. Since then none of the authorities had had reason to concern themselves with Fransson other than as a matter of routine. He had drawn his national pension and had kept to himself. He had subscribed to the *Småland Gazette* since the early 1950s.

'What's agoraphobia?' Gunvald Larsson asked.

'Morbid dread of public places,' Melander said.

Investigation headquarters were buzzing with activity. Every available man had been put on to the job. Most of them had forgotten their tiredness. Hope of a quick solution had been kindled.

Outside, the weather grew slowly colder. A light rain had begun to fall.

Information poured in as though on a teleprinter. The police as yet had no photograph, but they did have a complete description, the missing details having been filled in by doctors, neighbours, former workmates and the assistants in the shops where he bought his food.

Fransson was 5 feet 8 inches tall, weighed about twelve and a half stone and, sure enough, took size 8 in shoes.

The neighbours said that he spoke little but was a gentle and friendly man who always passed the time of day. He had a Småland accent. Seemed the sort of person you could trust. No one had seen him for eight days.

The technicians in the flat at Sveavägen had by this time checked and examined everything possible. There seemed no doubt that Fransson had committed both murders. They had even found blood on the black shoe in the cupboard.

'So he lay low for more than ten years,' Kollberg said.

'And now he's got the itch and wanders about raping and murdering little girls,' Gunvald Larsson said.

A telephone rang. Rönn answered.

Martin Beck paced up and down, biting his knuckles.

'We know practically everything that's worth knowing about him,' he said. 'We have everything except his photograph. And I expect that will turn up too. The only thing we don't know is – where is he now?'

'I know where he was fifteen minutes ago,' Rönn said. 'A dead girl is lying in St Erik's Park.'

28

St Erik's Park is one of the smallest in the city; in fact it is so insignificant that most Stockholmers don't even know of its existence. Few people go there and still fewer have any thought of guarding it.

It lies in the northern part of the city, forming a kind of unnatural end to the long street of Västmannagatan. A small tree-covered rocky outcrop with gravel paths and steps, pitching down rather steeply towards the surrounding streets. The greater part of the area is, moreover, occupied by a school, which of course is closed in the summer.

The body lay in the north-west part of the park, fully visible and right out on the edge of the rock. It was a macabre corroboration of the theory that the murders would get more and more horrible. The man called Ingemund Fransson had been in a great hurry this time. He had bashed the girl's head against a stone and strangled her. Then he had ripped open her red plastic coat and her dress, torn her panties off and rammed something resembling the shaft of an old hammer up between her legs.

To make matters worse, it was the girl's mother who had found her. The girl, whose name was Solveig, was older than the previous victims, having already turned eleven. She lived in Dannemoragatan, less than five minutes' walk from the scene of the crime, and, as far as anyone knew, she had had no reason to be in the park at all. She had gone out to buy some chocolate at a sweet kiosk almost on the corner of Dannemoragatan and Norra Stationsgatan, outside the actual park and at its north-east end. The errand should not have taken more than ten minutes and the girl had been told several times previously not to play in the park, which in any case she was not in the habit of doing. When she had been gone only a quarter of an hour her mother had gone out to look for her. She would have gone with her at the outset if she had not had another daughter, who was only eighteen months old and had to be looked after. She had found the body almost at once, had broken down completely and was already in the hospital.

They stood in the bleak drizzle gazing down at the dead child, feeling far more guilty than the perpetrator of this death, so hideous and pointless. The panties could not be found, nor the chocolate. Perhaps Ingemund Fransson was hungry and had taken it with him.

No doubt that it was his work. There was even a witness, who had seen him standing and talking to the girl. But they had seemed on such familiar terms that the witness was convinced that he saw a father who was out with his daughter. Ingemund Fransson was, as they knew, gentle and friendly and seemed the sort of person you could trust. He had been dressed in a beige-coloured corduroy jacket, brown trousers, white shirt open at the neck, and neat black shoes.

The missing panties were light blue.

'He must be somewhere close by,' Kollberg said.

Below them, the heavy traffic rumbled past on the main thoroughfare along St Eriksgatan and Norra Stationsgatan. Martin Beck gazed out over the sprawling railway depot and said quietly:

'Comb every railway carriage, every warehouse, every cellar, every attic in this area. Now. Immediately.'

Then he turned and walked away. The time was three o'clock on Tuesday 20 June. It was raining.

29

The hunt began about five o'clock on Tuesday afternoon; it was still going on at midnight and was intensified during the early morning hours.

Every single man who could be spared for the search was on the go, every dog was out and every car in movement. The hunt was concentrated at first on the northern parts of the city but spread by degrees to the centre and then out to the suburbs.

Stockholm is a city in which many thousands of people sleep out of doors in the summer. Not only tramps, junkies and alcoholics but also a large number of visitors who cannot get hotel rooms and just as many homeless people who, though fit for work and for the most part capable of holding down a job, cannot find anywhere to live, since bungled community planning has resulted in an acute housing shortage. They sleep on park benches and on old newspapers spread out on the ground, under bridges, on quaysides and in back yards. An equal number find temporary lodging in condemned houses, in buildings under construction, in air-raid shelters, garages, carriages, staircases, cellars, attics and sheds. Or in coastal vessels and motorboats and old wrecks. Many drift about in the ground stations and at the railway station or climb into some athletic field, and those who are streetwise have no great difficulty in getting down into the subterranean communications system beneath the big city buildings with its labyrinth of corridors and connecting shafts.

Plainclothes and uniformed policemen shook thousands of such people awake on this night, forcing them to their feet, shining torches into faces stupid with sleep and demanding proof of identity. Many came in for this five or six times; they moved about from place to place, only to be prodded awake by new police who were just as exhausted as themselves.

Otherwise the streets were quiet. Not even prostitutes and drug pushers dared to show their faces; evidently they did not realize that the police had less time for them than ever.

By seven o'clock on Wednesday morning the hunt had died down. Haggard and hollow-eyed policemen stumbled home for a few hours' sleep, others dropped like felled trees on to sofas and wooden benches in the guardrooms and dayrooms of the various stations.

Scores of people were found that night, in the most surprising places, but none of them was called Ingemund Rudolf Fransson.

At seven o'clock Kollberg and Martin Beck were at headquarters at Kungsholmsgatan. By now they were so tired that they were past feeling it and had got their second wind, as it were.

Kollberg was standing with his hands behind his back in front of the big map on the wall.

'He was a gardening labourer,' he said. 'Employed by the local council. He worked for eight years in the city parks, he must have got to know them all during that time. And up to now he hasn't gone outside the actual city limits. He keeps to ground he knows.'

'If only we could be sure,' Martin Beck said.

'One thing is certain. He didn't sleep in any park last night. Not in Stockholm.'

Kollberg paused and said reflectively:

'Unless we've had damn bad luck.'

'Exactly,' Martin Beck said. 'Besides, there are enormous areas that just can't be checked effectively at night. Djurgården, Gärdet, Lill-Jans Wood . . . to say nothing of the districts outside the city.'

'The Nacka reserve,' Kollberg said.

'The cemeteries,' Martin Beck said.

'Yes, the cemeteries . . . They're locked, it's true, but . . .'

Martin Beck looked at the clock.

'The immediate question is: what does he do in the daytime?'

'That's what is so fantastic,' Kollberg said. 'He evidently walks around town quite openly.'

'We've got to pull him in today,' Martin Beck said. 'Anything else is unthinkable.'

'Yes,' Kollberg said.

The psychologists were on the alert and came forward with the view that Ingemund Fransson was not deliberately trying to hide or keep out of the way. He was probably in a state of nonconsciousness but acted, also unconsciously, in an intelligent way and with automatic instinct of self-preservation.

'Very enlightening,' Kollberg said.

A little later Gunvald Larsson arrived. He had been working independently and along lines of his own.

'Do you know how far I've driven since last evening? Three hundred and forty kilometres. In this damn city. And slowly. I think he must be some kind of spook.'

'That's one way of looking at it,' Kollberg said.

Melander also had a point of view.

'The systematics disturb me. He commits one murder and then another almost immediately afterwards, then there's an interval of eight days, then a new murder and now . . .'

All had points of view.

The public was hysterical and panic-stricken and the police force overworked.

The general review of the situation on Wednesday morning had an air of optimism and confidence. On the surface. Deep down inside each man was just as afraid as the next.

'We need more men,' Hammar said. 'Get every available man from the outlying districts. Many will volunteer.'

And plainclothes men, that was a recurrent theme. Plainclothes police in key places; everyone who had a track suit or old overalls was to take himself out into the bushes.

'We must have a lot of uniformed men on patrol,' Martin Beck said. 'To reassure the public. To give them a sense of security.'

Thinking of what he had just said, he was overcome by a bitter feeling of hopelessness and helplessness.

'Compulsory proof of identity in all licences,' Hammar said.

That was a good idea, but it did not lead to any results.

Nothing seemed to lead anywhere. The hours of Wednesday dragged past. A dozen or so alarms were received but none of them seemed very hopeful and all turned out in fact to be false.

Evening came, and a chilly night. The raids continued.

Nobody slept. Gunvald Larsson drove another three hundred kilometres at 46 öre a kilometre.

'The dogs are groggy too,' he said when he came back. 'They're even past biting policemen.'

The morning of Thursday, 22 June gave prospects of a warm but windy day.

'I'm going up to Skansen to stand there disguised as a maypole,' Gunvald Larsson said.

No one had the energy to answer him. Martin Beck felt sick and his stomach heaved. When he tried to hold the paper mug to his lips his hand shook so much that he spilled coffee on Melander's blotting paper. And Melander, who was otherwise very finicky, didn't even seem to notice.

Melander was also unusually grave. He was thinking of the timetable. The timetable which showed that it was almost time for the next.

At two o'clock in the afternoon release came at last. In the form of a telephone call. Rönn answered.

'Where? In Djurgården?'

Putting his hand over the mouthpiece, he looked at the others and said:

'He's in Djurgården. Several persons have seen him.'

'If we're lucky he's still in South Djurgården, and then we've got him cornered,' Kollberg said in the car as they drove east, closely followed by Melander and Rönn.

South Djurgården is an island and to get there one must cross one of the two bridges across Djurgårdsbrunnsviken and the canal, unless one takes the ferry or has a boat of one's own. On the third of the island nearest to the centre of town are museums, the amusement park of Gröna Lund, summer restaurants, motor-boat and yacht clubs, Skansen's open-air museum and zoo, and the residential district, like a small village, known as Gamla Djurgårdsstaden. The rest of its area is covered with cultivated parkland interspersed with woods. The buildings are old but well preserved: manor houses, mansions, dignified villas and small eighteenth-century wooden houses dotted about, all surrounded by beautiful gardens.

Melander and Rönn turned off on to the Djurgården bridge while Kollberg and Martin Beck drove straight on to the Djurgården Inn. A few police cars were already drawn up in front of the restaurant.

The bridge over the canal was cordoned off by a radio patrol car and on the other side they saw another police car driving slowly in the direction of the Manilla deaf-and-dumb school.

A small cluster of people stood at the north end of the bridge. As Martin Beck and Kollberg approached, an elderly man detached himself from the group and went up to them.

'I take it you're the superintendents,' he said.

They stopped and Martin Beck nodded.

'My name's Nyberg,' the man went on. 'I was the one who discovered the murderer and called the police.'

'Where did you find him?' Martin Beck asked.

'Below Gröndal. He was standing in the road looking up at the house. I recognized him at once from the picture and description in the papers. At first I didn't know what to do, whether to try and nab him, but as I got closer I heard him talking to himself. It sounded so odd that I knew he must be dangerous, so I walked up to the inn as quietly as possible and phoned the police.'

'Talking to himself, was he,' Kollberg remarked. 'Did you hear what he said?'

'He stood there saying he was ill. He expressed himself in a very funny way, but that's what he said. That he was ill. When I'd phoned I went back but he had gone. Then I kept watch here by the bridge until the police came.'

Martin Beck and Kollberg went on down to the bridge and spoke to the radio policemen.

The man had been seen by several witnesses between the canal and Manilla, and the witness at Gröndal was obviously the last one to have seen him. As the area had been cordoned off so quickly there was every reason to believe that the man was still in South Djurgården. No bus had crossed the bridge after the witness saw the man at Gröndal. The roads into town had been closed immediately and the man could hardly have got as far as Skansen or Djurgårdsstaden before that. There was not much chance of taking him by surprise, he must already have noticed that the police were out in full force.

Martin Beck and Kollberg got into their car and drove across the bridge, closely followed by two prowl cars. They stopped on the road between the deaf-and-dumb school and the bridge and started to organize the hunt from there.

A quarter of an hour later all available men from several of Stockholm's police districts had arrived on the scene and about a hundred policemen had been sent out to cover the area between Skansen and Blockhusudden.

Martin Beck sat in the car directing the search by radio. The search groups were equipped with walkie-talkies and the roads were patrolled by squad cars. Dozens of innocent pedestrians were stopped time and again, forced to prove their identity and told to leave the area. At the roadblocks all cars on their way into town were stopped and checked.

In the park by Rosendal Manor a young man broke into a run when a policeman asked to see his identity card and in panic he ran right into the arms of two other policemen. He refused to say who he was and why he had run. When they searched him they found a loaded 9-millimetre Parabellum in his coat pocket and he was taken straight to the nearest police station.

'In this way we'll soon have pulled in every criminal in Stockholm except the one we want,' Kollberg said.

'He's lying low somewhere,' said Martin Beck. 'This time he can't escape.'

'Don't be so sure. We can't keep the area cordoned off indefinitely. And if he has got past Skansen . . .'

'He didn't have time. Unless he drove a car and that doesn't seem likely.'

'Why not? He might have stolen one,' Kollberg said.

A voice crackled on the radio. Martin Beck pressed the button and answered.

'Car ninety-seven, nine seven, here. We've found him. Over.'

'Where are you?' Martin Beck asked.

'At Biskopsudden. Above the boat club.'

'We'll be right over.'

It took them three minutes to drive to Biskopsudden. Three radio cars, a motorcycle policeman and several plainclothes and uniformed policemen were standing in the road. Between the cars and surrounded by the police stood the man. A radio policeman in a leather jacket was holding his arm bent behind his back.

The man was thin and somewhat shorter than Martin Beck. He had a big nose, blue-grey eyes, and sandy hair brushed back and rather thin on top. He was dressed in brown trousers, white shirt with no tie, and dark-brown jacket. As Martin Beck and Kollberg came towards him he said:

'What's all this?'

'What's your name?' Martin Beck asked.

'Fristedt. Wilhelm Fristedt.'

'Can you prove your identity?'

'No, my driver's licence is in the pocket of another coat.'

'Where have you been during the last two weeks?'

'Nowhere. I mean at home. In Bondegatan. I've been ill.'

'Alone at home?'

It was Kollberg who asked. He sounded sarcastic.

'Yes,' the man replied.

'Your name's Fransson, isn't it?' Martin Beck said kindly.

'No, it's Fristedt. Must he grip my arm so tightly? It hurts.'

Martin Beck nodded to the policeman in the leather jacket.

'Okay. Put him in the car.'

He and Kollberg moved to one side and Martin Beck said:

'What do you think? Is it our man?'

Kollberg scratched his head.

'I don't know. He seems so neat and ordinary. But his appearance tallies and he has no proof of identity. I don't know.'

Martin Beck went up to the car and opened the door to the rear seat.

'What are you doing here in Djurgården?'

'Nothing. Just out for a walk. What's all this about?'

'And you can't prove your identity?'

'No, unfortunately.'

'Where do you live?'

'In Bondegatan. Why are you asking me all this?'

'What were you doing last Tuesday?'

'The day before yesterday? I was at home. I was ill. Today's the first time I've been out in over two weeks.'

'Who can prove it?' Martin Beck asked. 'Was anyone with you when you were ill?'

'No, I was alone.'

Martin Beck drummed on the car roof and looked at Kollberg. Kollberg opened the door on the other side, leaned into the car and said:

'May I ask what it was you said when you were over by Gröndal half an hour ago?'

'I beg your pardon?'

'You said something when you stood below Gröndal earlier today.'

'Oh!' the man said. 'Oh, that.'

He smiled and said:

'I am the sick lime-tree that withers while still young.
Dry leaves I scattered to the wind when on my
 crown they hung.

'Is that what you mean?'

The policeman in the leather jacket was gaping at the man.

'Fröding,' Kollberg said.

'Yes,' the man said. 'Our great poet Fröding. He was living at Gröndal when he died. Not so old but out of his mind.'

'What's your job?' Martin Beck asked.

'I'm a butcher,' the man replied.

Martin Beck straightened up and looked at Kollberg over the car roof. Kollberg shrugged. Martin Beck lit a cigarette and inhaled deeply. Then he bent down and looked at the man.

'Okay,' he said. 'Let's start again. What's your name?'

The sun beat down on the car roof. The man in the back seat mopped his brow and said:

'Wilhelm Fristedt.'

30

One might take Martin Beck for a country bumpkin and Kollberg for a sex murderer. One could put a false beard on Rönn and get someone to believe he was Santa Claus, and a confused witness might say that Gunvald Larsson was Chinese. One could no doubt dress up the assistant commissioner as a labourer and the commissioner as a tree. One could probably persuade someone that the minister for home affairs was a policeman. One could, like the Japanese during the Second World War and certain monomaniac photographers, disguise oneself as a bush and make pretence at not being found out. One could hoodwink people about almost anything at all.

But nothing in this world could make people be mistaken about Kristiansson and Kvant.

Kristiansson and Kvant were dressed in uniform caps and leather jackets with gilded buttons. Their belts were attached to straps diagonally across their chests and they carried pistols and truncheons. Their dress was due to the fact that they felt cold as soon as the temperature dropped below seventy degrees.

They were both from the province of Skåne, in the far south.

Both were six foot two and had blue eyes. Both were broad-shouldered and fair-haired and weighed about thirteen stone. They drove a black Plymouth with white mudguards. It had a search-light and radio mast, a rotating orange flashlight and two red lights on the roof. In addition, the word POLICE was painted in white block letters in four places: over the doors, on the hood and across the back.

Kristiansson and Kvant were radio police.

Before joining the force they had both been regular sergeants in the South Skåne Infantry Regiment at Ystad.

Both were married and each had two children.

They had worked together for a long time and knew each other as well as only two men in a radio car can do. They applied for transfer at the same time and got on badly with everyone except each other.

Yet they were not really alike and they often got on each other's nerves. Kristiansson was gentle and conciliatory, Kvant hot-tempered and truculent. Kristiansson never mentioned his wife, Kvant talked of hardly anything else but his. By this time Kristiansson knew everything about her; not only what she said and did, but the most intimate details regarding her body and general behaviour.

They were regarded as complementing each other perfectly.

They had pulled in many thieves and thousands of drunks and they had put a stop to hundreds of domestic rows; Kvant had even started a few rows himself, since he took it for granted that people always got noisy and troublesome when they suddenly found two policemen standing in their hall.

They had never made a spectacular scoop of any kind or had their names in the papers. Once, while serving in Malmö, they had driven a drunken journalist, who was murdered six months later, to the casualty department of the hospital. He had cut his wrists. This was the nearest they had ever come to fame.

The radio car was their second home, with its faint reek of alco-holic fumes left by all the drunks and with its atmosphere, hard to define, of stale intimacy.

Some people thought they were stuck-up because they spoke with a Skåne accent, and they themselves were annoyed when certain persons with no feeling for the sound and quality of the dialect tried to mimic them.

Kristiansson and Kvant did not even belong to the Stockholm police. They were radio police in Solna, outside the city boundary, and knew very little more about the park murders than what they had read in the papers and heard on the radio.

Soon after half past two on Thursday, 22 June they were right in front of the military academy at Karlberg, with only twenty minutes of their shift to go.

Kristiansson, who was at the wheel, had just reversed the car on the old parade ground and was now driving westwards along Karlberg Strand.

'Stop a moment,' Kvant said.

'Why?'

'I want to have a look at that boat.'

After a while Kristiansson said with a yawn:

'Had a good look?'

'Yes.'

They drove on slowly.

'The park murderer has been caught,' Kristiansson said. 'They've got him surrounded at Djurgården.'

'So I heard,' Kvant said.

'Good thing the kids are down in Skåne.'

'Yes. Funny thing, you know . . .'

He broke off. Kristiansson said nothing.

'Funny thing,' Kvant went on. 'Before I married Siv I was always after the girls. One bird after the other, couldn't stop. Virile, as they say. In fact, I was a randy devil.'

'Yes, I remember,' Kristiansson said, yawning.

'But now – why, now I feel like an old horse that's been put out to graze. Fall dead asleep the minute I get into bed. And all I think of when I wake up is cornflakes and milk.'

He made a short, pregnant pause and added:

'Must be old age creeping on.'

Kristiansson and Kvant had just turned thirty.

'Yes,' Kristiansson said.

He drove past Karlberg bridge and was now only twenty-five yards from the city boundary. Had the park murderer not been surrounded at Djurgården he would probably have swung up to the right to Ekelundsvågen and had a look at what was left of the woods there after the new blocks of flats had gone up. But there was no reason to now, and anyway he'd rather not see the National Police College twice in the same day if he could help it. So he continued westwards along the winding road by the water.

They drove past Talludden and Kvant looked sourly at the teenagers hanging about outside the café and around the cars in the car park.

'By rights we ought to stop and take a look at their old rust buckets.'

'That's the traffic boys' headache,' Kristiansson said. 'We're due back at the station in fifteen minutes.'

They sat for a while in silence.

'Good thing they've pulled in that sex maniac,' Kristiansson said.

'If only you could once say something I haven't heard twenty times already.'

'It's not so easy.'

'Siv was in a stinking temper this morning,' Kvant said. 'Did I tell you about that lump she thought she had on her left breast? The one she thought might be cancer?'

'Yes, you did.'

'Oh. Well, anyway, I thought now she's been nagging so long about that lump so I'll have a good feel myself. She was lying there like a dead fish when the alarm went off and of course I woke up before she did. So I . . .'

'Yes, you told me.'

They had come to the end of Karlberg Strand, but instead of turning up towards the Sundbyberg road – which was the shortest way to the police station – Kristiansson drove straight on and along Huvudsta Allé, a road seldom used by anybody nowadays.

Later, many people were to ask him why he took that particular road, but that was a question he could not answer. He just took it, and that was that. In any case, Kvant did not react. He had been a radio policeman far too long to ask useless questions. Instead, he said thoughtfully:

'No, I just can't make out what has got into her. Siv, I mean.'

They passed Huvudsta Castle.

Not much of a castle, come to that, Kristiansson thought for perhaps the five-hundredth time. At home in Skåne there are real castles. With counts and barons in them. Aloud he said:

'Can you lend me twenty kronor?'

Kvant nodded. Kristiansson was chronically short of money.

They drove slowly on. To the right lay a newly built residential area with tall apartment blocks, to the left was a narrow but densely wooded strip of land between the road and the Ulvsunda Lake.

'Stop a minute,' Kvant said.

'Why?'

'Call of nature.'

'We're nearly there.'

'Can't be helped.'

Kristiansson turned left and let the car glide slowly into one of the clearings. Then he stopped. Kvant got out and walked around the car, over to some low bushes, placed his legs wide apart and whistled as he pulled down the zipper of his fly. He looked over the bushes. Then he turned his head and saw a man standing only five or six yards away, evidently on the same business as himself.

'Sorry,' Kvant said, turning politely the other way.

He adjusted his clothes and went towards the car. Kristiansson had opened the door and sat there looking out.

While still two yards from the car Kvant stopped dead and said:

'But that man looked like . . . and behind was sitting . . .'

At the same time Kristiansson said:

'I say, that fellow there . . .'

Kvant swung around and strode towards the man by the bushes. Kristiansson started to get out of the car.

The man was dressed in a beige-coloured corduroy jacket, grubby white shirt, crumpled brown trousers and black shoes. He was of medium height, with a big nose and thin hair brushed straight back. And he had still not adjusted his clothes.

When Kvant was only two yards from him the man raised his right arm to his face and said:

'Don't hit me.'

Kvant gave a start.

'What!' he said.

Only that morning his wife had told him he was a clumsy great lout and no one could help noticing it, but still, this was the limit. Controlling himself he said:

'What are you doing here?'

'Nothing,' the man said.

He gave a shy, awkward smile. Kvant eyed his clothes.

'Have you proof of identity?'

'Yes, I've my pension card in my pocket.'

Kristiansson came up to them. The man looked at him and said:

'Don't hit me.'

'Isn't your name Ingemund Fransson?' Kristiansson asked.

'Yes,' the man replied.

'I think you'd better come with us,' Kvant said, taking him by the arm.

The man willingly let himself be led over to the car.

'Get into the back seat,' Kristiansson said.

'And do up your fly,' Kvant ordered.

The man hesitated a moment. Then he smiled and obeyed. Kvant got into the back seat and sat beside him.

'Let's have a look at that pension card,' Kvant said.

The man put his hand into his hip pocket and drew out the pension warrant.

Kvant looked at it and passed it to Kristiansson.

'Doesn't seem any doubt,' Kristiansson said.

Kvant stared incredulously at the man and said:

'No, it's him all right.'

Kristiansson went around the car, opened the door on the other side and started going through the man's jacket pockets.

Now, at close range, he saw that the man's cheeks were sunken and that his chin was covered with grey stubble that must have been several days old.

'Here,' Kristiansson said, pulling something out of the inside pocket of the jacket.

It was a pair of little girls' panties, light blue.

'Hm. That settles it, doesn't it?' Kvant said. 'You've killed three little girls, haven't you? Eh?'

'Yes,' the man said.

He smiled and shook his head.

'I had to,' he said.

Kristiansson was still standing outside the car.

'How did you get them to go with you?' he asked.

'Oh, I've a way with children. Children always like me. I show them things. Flowers and so on.'

Kristiansson pondered for a moment. Then he said:

'Where did you sleep last night?'

'The northern cemetery,' the man said.

'Have you slept there all the time?' Kvant asked.

'No, in other cemeteries too. I don't really remember.'

'And in the daytime,' Kristiansson said. 'Where have you been in the daytime?'

'Oh, various places. In the churches a lot. It's so beautiful there. So quiet and still. You can sit there for hours . . .'

'But you made damn sure you didn't go home, didn't you, eh?' Kvant said.

'I did go once. I had got something on my shoes. And . . .'

'Yes?'

'I had to change them and put on my old trainers. Then of course I bought new shoes. Very expensive. Outrageously expensive, I don't mind saying.'

Kristiansson and Kvant stared at him.

'And then I fetched my jacket.'

'I see,' said Kristiansson.

'It really gets quite chilly when you have to sleep out of doors at night,' the man said conversationally.

They heard the sound of quick footsteps, and a young woman in a blue smock and wooden-soled shoes came running along. She caught sight of the radio car and stopped dead.

'Oh,' she said, panting. 'I suppose you haven't . . . My little girl . . . I can't find her . . . I turned my back for a few minutes and she was gone. You haven't seen her, have you? She is wearing a red dress . . .'

Kvant wound the window down to say something. Then he thought better of it and said politely:

'Yes, madam. She's sitting behind the bushes over there playing with a doll. She's all right. I saw her a few moments ago.'

Kristiansson instinctively kept the light-blue panties behind his back and tried to smile at the woman. The result was horrible.

'Not to worry,' he said feebly.

The woman ran over to the bushes and a moment later they heard a little girl's clear voice:

'Hello, Mummy!'

Ingemund Fransson's features flattened out and his eyes grew dull and staring.

Kvant gripped his arm tightly and said:

'Let's get moving, Kalle.'

Kristiansson banged the door, climbed into the driver's seat and started the engine. As he backed up towards the road he said:

'I'm just wondering . . .'

'What?' Kvant asked.

'Who's the man they've pulled in at Djurgården?'

'Hell, yes, I wonder ...' Kvant said.

'Please don't grip so hard,' said the man called Ingemund Fransson. 'You're hurting me.'

'Shut up,' said Kvant.

Martin Beck was still standing at Biskopsudden in Djurgården, almost five miles from Huvudsta Allé. He stood quite still, chin in hand, looking at Kollberg, who was red in the face and sweating all over. A motorcycle policeman in a white helmet and with a walkie-talkie on his back had just saluted and roared off.

Two minutes earlier Melander and Rönn had driven the man who said his name was Fristedt home to Bondegatan to give him a chance of proving his identity. But this was only a formality. Neither Martin Beck nor Kollberg doubted any longer that they had been on the wrong track.

Only one radio car was left. Kollberg was standing by the open door near the driver, Martin Beck a few yards away.

'Here's something,' said the man in the radio car. 'Something on the radio.'

'What?' Kollberg asked glumly.

The policeman listened.

'A radio patrol at Solna.'

'Well?'

'They've caught him.'

'Fransson?'

'Yes, they've got him in the car.'

Martin Beck came up. Kollberg bent down to hear better.

'What are they saying?' Martin Beck asked.

'No doubt whatever,' said the man in the radio car. 'Identity established. He has even confessed. What's more he had a pair of little girl's light-blue panties in his pocket. Caught red-handed.'

'What!' Kollberg exclaimed. 'Red-handed? Has he ...'

'No, they got there in time. The girl's unharmed.'

Martin Beck leaned his forehead against the edge of the car roof. The metal was hot and dusty.

'Good God, Lennart,' he said, 'it's over.'

'Yes,' Kollberg replied. 'For this time.'

Ideas,
interviews
& features . . .

Sex in the City

by Richard Shephard

IN THEIR THIRD Martin Beck novel, Sjöwall and Wahlöö have really begun to hit their stride. While the first two books saw the pair affording us a glimpse of a Sweden in the throes of collapse, here they depict a country that's ineluctably corrupt and rapidly imploding, the victim of its own moral decay. Moving forward roughly twelve months from the events in *The Man Who Went Up in Smoke*, they have underlined their highly potent message by shrewdly setting the novel in 1967, the year of the so-called summer of love. But while the hippie dream may have wafted blissfully over to Sweden, settling in Stockholm, it has transmogrified en route into a hideous nightmare, with its rose-coloured cloud of incense now a gloomy miasma of drug addiction, petty crime and prostitution. In their cool, unflinching appraisal of the country and its inhabitants, memorably described by Beck's colleague and friend, Kollberg, as 'the swift gangsterization of this society', there is clearly no such thing as *free* love. In fact it looks as if love has left the party altogether. In its wake has sidled sex, in its seamiest and most sordid incarnations. From the outset, Beck, now a superintendent, is propositioned at Stockholm's Central station by a teenage girl, who 'looked the same age as his daughter', and who tries to sell him photographs of herself unencumbered by such bourgeois trappings as underwear, with 'her dress up to her armpits'. Beck merely calls over to a couple of station policemen and wanders off, musing that 'some idiot was sure to buy her photographs', thereby enabling her to 'buy purple hearts or marijuana . . . Or perhaps LSD.' Elsewhere in the novel, sex is on display throughout, ranging from a young couple carousing in a city park near the site of the first murder, to a young woman, Lisbeth, who is picked up when her consort for the night turns out to be a vicious mugger, sought by the police, or the perverse and lethal desires of the eponymous killer, a defiler and slayer of young girls.

The scene where Kollberg, already anxious because his wife is expecting their first baby while he is hunting for a child murderer, interviews Lisbeth in her apartment is both powerful and disturbing. Scantily clad, attractive, sexy and bold, she teases the policeman, who has to remind himself of his professional and marital obligations. As the interview progresses, the atmosphere heats up and the sexual tension between the two seems to drip from the page. Seductive, appealing and fully aware of the strength of her charms, Lisbeth casually tells Kollberg that she thinks he's 'very nice', to which he replies in similar fashion, before he suddenly turns to leave, informing her, almost apologetically and 'to his own astonishment', that he's married and a father-to-be, and that his life as a policeman can be 'dangerous'. With the spell disassembled, if not actually broken, by his reluctant display of will power, he drives off. Still distracted by his desire, he half-heartedly tries to convince himself that Lisbeth resembled his wife, before attempting to downplay the entire incident by telling ▶

Sex in the City *(continued)*

◄ himself that it's 'verging on the perfect parody of a really bad novel'.

Much darker than its predecessors, *The Man on the Balcony* finds Beck and his cohorts trying to catch two criminals – the mugger and their main quarry, a murderer who preys on very young girls, violating and then killing them. With the summer sun baking the city and causing tempers and passions to flare, the police desperately struggle to track down the killer before another young victim is sacrificed. They have two possible witnesses to the first crime, but neither is particularly reliable. One is a three-year-old boy, and the other is the aforementioned mugger.

If the second Martin Beck novel was redolent of the Alfred Hitchcock films of the 1950s, then *The Man on the Balcony* has echoes of Austrian director Fritz Lang's 1931 masterpiece, *M*. Like that film, the atmosphere inside a police station is superbly evoked, with teams of harassed and chain-smoking officers working round the clock, their private lives, and perhaps their respiratory systems, left on hold. Although technological advances have been made and proceedings have accelerated since the snail-like rate of progress that was such a memorable feature in *Roseanna*, the police are still immersed in a constant and exhausting struggle, which is exacerbated by the fact, as Kollberg admits, that 'crime always seemed to be one step ahead'.

For most of *The Man on the Balcony*, it would appear that crime is so many steps ahead it's left the officers blinded by its dust. Computers and modern methods, helpful as they are, seem to mock the police with their impersonal functionality. When Kollberg has completed the awful task of breaking the terrible news to the mother of her little girl's death and he's left her in the care of her doctor, he reflects bitterly on the general efficacy of the new equipment and systems before ruefully acknowledging 'what little consolation these excellent technical inventions had to offer' the bereaved woman who, tragically, cannot even bring herself to admit that her daughter is really dead. In a poignant moment, he also includes himself and his fellow officers – 'the set-faced men who had now gathered round the little body in the bushes' – amongst those who need to be consoled.

The main parallel with *M*, however, is that the principal crime, the sexual abuse and murder of little girls, is essentially the same, and there are similarities in the respective captures of the murderers. In Lang's film, set in Berlin, the killer is tracked down and eventually caught by more 'normal' criminals obliged to do the policemen's job for them. In *The Man on the Balcony* the arrest is largely due to the intervention of wrongdoers. Chief among them is the description given to Beck and his crew by the mugger, a felon who is himself caught because he's been informed on by a spurned prostitute. Motivated by a goal as mundane as profit and their shallow desire to earn their livelihood through robbery and assault or sex, the pair's misdeeds are vastly overshadowed by those of the killer, whose compulsions inhabit a terrain too dark and dangerous to explore. This was fertile territory for Lang, whose entire career seemed to consist of such sombre probing, but it appears to ▶

Sex in the City *(continued)*

◀ be equally productive for Sjöwall and Wahlöö.

Much of the novels' impact comes from the contrast between the policemen's private and professional lives and in *The Man on the Balcony* this is brought to the fore by Kollberg, who nervously awaits the birth of his child, his anxiety sharply opposed to the maternal serenity of his wife. She slumbers blissfully, stirring slightly while their unborn child kicks, and is watched over by her husband as he lies next to her, too tired and careworn to fall asleep. The incident with Lisbeth, the sexy interviewee, has raised the difference between police life and everyday life. Which does Kollberg prefer: cosy domesticity and parenthood, or the chance of danger and excitement and arousing encounters with women like Lisbeth? Later, after he is attacked by two clumsy vigilante types and gets into bed bruised and aching, he asks his wife to hold him, but she only does so after replying that her 'tummy's in the way', as if the baby, not even yet born, has already started coming between them.

The choice between lingering in the parlour and heading for the police station is similarly confronted by Beck, whose private life, rarely on display in the second book, now appears to have receded even further from view. There's so little of it on display, in fact, that it scarcely seems to exist. At the close of the previous book, his holiday, interrupted by his being asked to solve the case of the missing journalist, is resumed, but now his heart has gone out of it. Here, the story begins with him on holiday again, a year later, but this time it's a kind of working holiday and he is alone and visiting his friend and fellow police officer, Gunnar Ahlberg, in Motala, the setting for *Roseanna*. Beck's wife, Inga, more of a dominant presence in that first novel, is mostly reduced to a few short cameos, one of them merely as a hectoring voice on the telephone, a role that she performs with aplomb.

In the other brief scenes with her, Beck first has 'a violent quarrel', of which the subject is 'so trivial' he can't even remember it, and then later on, aware 'that a quarrel was blowing up', he hurries through his breakfast and quickly leaves for work, his eagerness to get away suggesting that even *his* hellish job, with all its pressures and privations, offers some kind of sanctuary from, and is preferable to, the binding ties of married life. And in a perfectly delineated bit of irony, while Stockholm's saucy citizens, possibly along with the rest of Sweden, seem to be giving in to all manner of sexual temptation, Beck and his wife are markedly unswayed by such enticements. Returning home exhausted from work early one morning, he finds his wife in bed, naked. 'Does it get you all excited perhaps?' she waspishly asks him, but he is already asleep, his last waking thought being the decision to buy a divan for himself 'and put it in the other room', away from her troublesome presence.

In stark relief to this uxorious vacuum is the warm relationship between Beck and Kollberg, a bond forged by countless shared experiences in their years of working together, and one that, since it consists mostly of lengthy silences punctuated by significant glances and the odd remark, is virtually telepathic. As if to ▶

Sex in the City *(continued)*

◀ underline the symbiotic nature of their friendship, as well as the difficulties of their job, the two policemen are shown to be equally 'aware of their powerlessness and of their ambivalent attitude to the society they were there to protect'. For such diligent and dedicated men, chatter is idle, and there is really no place for it in their day, a point slyly confirmed by Sjöwall and Wahlöö, who usually preface a description of their characters' activities with the phrase 'without a word'.

As the sun pours down and another young girl is tragically added to the growing list of victims, bringing more sorrow to grieving parents and harassed policemen, more headlines and more pressures, Beck is increasingly irritated by a dim recollection of something, an incident forgotten and discarded by everybody else, but which will bring about the turning point in their efforts to crack the case. Again and again he prods his overworked brain, trying to recall the errant detail, sure that it could make all the difference. Other factors in the investigation seem to approach it too, as if they are trying to envelop it in their orbit and expose it, but still it continues to elude him, so that, like Kollberg, he cannot summon up any much needed sleep, and instead lies 'awake in the dark, thinking. Of something.' As with the bureaucratic impediments and logistic longueurs in *Roseanna*, a kind of suspense is gradually amassed here as the reader, with a delicious sense of impatience, waits for the light bulb above Beck's head to finally be illuminated.

When this occurs, nearly three-quarters of the way through the novel, the stymied, frustrated policeman feels 'a wave of warmth pass through him', the kind of sensation that his sixteen-year marriage has long seemed incapable of inspiring. But after this moment, the pace picks up sharply, and, though the police are stretched, exhausted and overworked, Beck's timely *aperçu* spurs them into a welter of frenzied activity, and a huge hunt takes place, systematically spreading out over Stockholm, turning the picturesque city into a setting for a *noir* film, and once again echoing Lang's *M*. Ironically, street crime is temporarily on the wane, with 'not even prostitutes and drug pushers' surfacing, since they remain unaware that 'the police had less time for them than ever'.

Finally, aided by an instance of dumb luck, the police have their killer, catching him just as he is preparing to strike again, and the novel concludes with the explosive sense of relief expressed by the police that the horror is over, a sense gently tempered by Kollberg, who mutters, 'For this time'.

Akin to the manhunt that gradually engulfs the city, Sjöwall and Wahlöö's master plan, in this third novel, has begun to take solid shape. The stage is set; the characters are all in place and, while the authors' portrayal of the policemen, their personalities, procedures and private lives is certainly fascinating, what is really compelling and remains the highlight of the series – or Beckalogue, perhaps – is the unswerving progress of their brilliant and artfully assembled portrayal of Sweden and its society. With their fourth offering, *The Laughing Policeman*, they raise the stakes considerably but take no prisoners. ∎

Further Interrogation of Maj Sjöwall

Q and A by Richard Shephard

The third novel is set in the summer of 1967, the summer of love, and there seemed to be more drugs, long hair, sex and a general air of decadence. Presumably, Stockholm and the rest of Sweden fell under the spell of the hippies' influence. Did you set out to portray this?
We were a little too old and busy doing other things to be hippies, but from time to time we lived in left-wing communities. My daughter Lena (born in 1956) was living together with an American deserter and they were definitely hippies during their young years. We had no particular intention of portraying that time period; it was all around us at the time we wrote the book.

You have portrayed this period, despite its much vaunted liberalism, as being fairly squalid and full of dire consequences – addiction, prostitution, etc. Was this view just seen from Beck's perspective or did you regard this time as an unpleasant, irresponsible one?
There was a big difference between the so-called hippie communities and the growing drug environment. Hippies grew and smoked marijuana at the most, were often sober, vegetarians, down-to-earth and environmentally conscious. Narcotics entered the criminal environment and created new problems. The attitudes towards this as shown in the books are probably mostly seen through the eyes of the police.

The case is solved really only after Beck has finally remembered Larsson's phone call with the old lady. Was this because you wanted to show that Beck would get there in the end, or to keep the reader in suspense, or even to show that Larsson was brash and inclined to be rather careless?

The fact that Gunvald Larsson's phone call was remembered later in the story was, I think, mostly a way of building suspense, and not really a characterization of Larsson.

The killer in the novel preys on young girls. Was there an actual killer in Sweden at the time, or did you invent this? The infamous Moors Murderers in England were only a few years earlier than this, for example.

There had been a sexual offender in Stockholm prior to us writing the book. Without being conscious of it, that story rather functioned as a model for our book through faintly remembered newspaper articles, but we didn't purposely use the case.

We had read about the Moors Murderers, of course, but we hadn't particularly had them in mind. The English case was completely different and, as far as I remember, a *folie à deux* case.

LIFE
at a Glance

Maj Sjöwall was born in 1935 in Stockholm, Sweden. She studied journalism and graphics and worked as a translator, as well as an art director and journalist for some of the most eminent magazines and newspapers in Sweden. She met her husband Per Wahlöö in 1961 through her work, and the two almost instantly became a couple. They had two sons together and, after the death of Per Wahlöö, Sjöwall continued to translate. She also wrote several short stories and the acclaimed crime novel *The Woman Who Resembled Greta Garbo*, with the Dutch crime writer Tomas Ross. She is arguably Sweden's finest translator and is still at work today.

Per Wahlöö (1926–1975) was born in Lund, Sweden. After graduating from ▶

The Next Titles in the Martin Beck Series

Critics have called the ten Martin Beck novels by Sjöwall and Wahlöö among the best in modern crime fiction.

....

The Laughing Policeman

On a cold and rainy Stockholm night, nine bus riders are gunned down by an unknown assassin. The press, anxious for an explanation for the seemingly random crime, quickly dubs him a madman. But Martin Beck of the Homicide Squad suspects otherwise: this apparently motiveless killer has managed to target one of Beck's best detectives – and he, surely, would not have been riding that lethal bus without a reason.

'A welcome addition to the Martin Beck casebook' Matthew Coady, *Guardian*

....

The Fire Engine That Disappeared

Gunvald Larsson sits carefully observing the dingy Stockholm apartment house of a man under police surveillance. He looks at his watch: nine minutes past eleven in the evening. He yawns, slapping his arms to keep warm. At the same moment the house explodes, killing at least three people. Chief Inspector Martin Beck and his men don't suspect arson or murder until they discover a peculiar circumstance and a link is established between the explosion and a suicide committed that same day, in which the dead man left a note consisting of just two words: Martin Beck.

'The book is extremely smoothly and skilfully written and you whiz through the pages like one o'clock' *The Times*

···

Murder at the Savoy

When Viktor Palmgren, a powerful industrialist, is casually shot during an after-dinner speech, the repercussions – both on the international money markets and on the residents of the small coastal town of Malmö – are widespread. Chief Inspector Martin Beck is called in to help catch a killer nobody, not even the victim, was able to identify. He begins a systematic search for the friends, enemies, business associates and call girls who may have wanted Palmgren dead – but in the process he finds to his dismay that he has nothing but contempt for the victim and sympathy for the murderer . . .

'Superior police procedural' *Guardian*

LIFE *at a Glance* *(continued)*

◀ the University of Lund, he worked as a journalist, covering criminal and social issues for a number of newspapers and magazines. In the 1950s Wahlöö was engaged in radical political causes and his activities resulted in his deportation from Franco's Spain in 1957. After returning to Sweden, he wrote a number of television and radio plays, and was the managing editor of several magazines, before becoming a full-time writer. Per Wahlöö died of cancer in 1975, only weeks after *The Terrorists*, the final instalment of the Martin Beck series, was published. ■

If You Loved This,
You Might Like . . .

The Dogs of Riga
by Henning Mankell
Like many of his books, Mankell's second
novel opens with a bizarre death, when two
corpses, frozen and sealed in a grisly tryst, are
washed up on a remote stretch of Sweden's
coastline in an inflatable dinghy. Having
ascertained that they're Eastern European
criminals and that they've probably been killed
in a gangland slaying, Inspector Kurt
Wallander crosses the Baltic Sea to Riga, in
Latvia, where he becomes involved in a deadly
international situation.

One Deadly Summer
by Sébastien Japrisot
Set in a small town in France and told in
multiple overlapping narrative strands,
Japrisot's novel is the story of Eliane, a
voluptuous and beautiful young woman with a
terrible secret and a deadly goal. Using her
ample charms, she seduces a young man and
then systematically tracks down three men in
his family in order to have revenge on them for
a crime committed twenty years earlier and
which they have seemingly buried. Passion,
tragedy, retribution and death run riot in this
steamy and powerful thriller.

The Devil's Star
by Jo Nesbo
This is the English debut from a Norwegian
writer who has already won the country's Glass
Key award for best crime novel. Set in the